I0642702

Under Guard

Royal House Series: Book 2

AE Moran

The Invisible Publishing Company

Contents

Chapter 1: Simone

I walk into the grand dining room and pause on the threshold to look around at all the guests, dignitaries, and ambassadors in expensive eveningwear.

Actually I don't walk into the grand dining room. I glide. My gown flares all the way down to the floor and hides my legs. I look like I'm floating across the floor.

I head over to French Ambassador Pierre LeGot and hold out my hand. "So good to see you again, Ambassador."

He bends over and kisses my knuckles. "The honor is all mine, Princess Simone. You look breathtaking tonight."

I pretend to look around. "My family is already here, I see."

"They are, indeed. Your new sister-in-law is stunning. Your brother made an excellent match—and they look so happy together."

"They are." I smile across the dining room at my brother Christophe's wife, Geneviève.

They stand side by side with her hand resting inside his elbow. They do look like the perfect couple. I never would have believed they could fall so madly in love after she started out as one of the Royal Family's deadliest enemies.

Geneviève smiles at everyone and gives me a knowing smirk when she catches my eye across the dining room.

I never thought I would make friends with one of the Royal Family's deadliest enemies, either, but I did. Geneviève is more than a friend now. She's a sister.

I only have one sister. Emeline stands on the other side of the room surrounded by handsome, young, adoring admirers all vying for her attention.

Emeline is the only sister I've ever had—until Geneviève came along.

I touch the ambassador on the arm. "Would you please excuse me? I need to go greet my father and mother."

He bows again. "Of course, Your Highness."

I glide across the room and meet up with my father and mother, Crown Prince Gustav and Princess Jasmine of Monaco.

My aunt Marguerite and her daughter, my cousin Johanne, stand next to my parents along with my two younger brothers, Pascal and Renáld.

I slide over next to my father and scan the room. "Everyone is here."

His eyes go hard when they dart from one cluster of guests to the other. He barely sees them.

Half the men here belong to our security team. My father, brothers, and our security team take extra precautions whenever we go anywhere in public, but no one can cover every possible contingency.

We've had too many security breaches and incidents of people trying to harm our family—especially the recent unpleasantness with Geneviève's family trying to wipe us all out in one blow.

The security guards wear immaculate tuxes just like everyone else here. Only one thing distinguishes the guards from everyone else. The guards wear earpieces in their ears with a coiled wire running behind their ears and down their shirt collars.

Oh, and none of the security guards brought a date. They're the only men here without women on their arms.

The guards' presence throws a bucket of cold water over the event. I can't tell if any other guests notice the guards, but my whole family becomes acutely aware of their presence.

Christophe and Geneviève talk, shake hands, and exchange pleasantries with guests coming over to greet them. Christophe and Geneviève smile as pleasantly as always. No one can put on the charm like Christophe.

He covers it up so well when his eyes flick around the room, too. He follows all the security guards' movements and activities, but none of his and Geneviève's admirers would ever have known.

Christophe takes charge of the Royal Family's security team. Every guard here answers to him, but that on its own poses a special problem. He can't be the head of security and one of the people the security team is supposed to be guarding at the same time.

I try to push that out of my mind and focus on just enjoying this state dinner. I get distracted by a bunch of dignitaries coming to greet me.

They're all handsome, male, and immaculately dressed and groomed. They pour on the charm, too. They all compliment me on my gown and tell me how beautiful I look tonight.

None of that means anything. I've been hearing that every night of my life. Every man on the planet wants to get up close and personal with one of the princesses of Monaco.

I blush and respond as politely as I can, but the tension coming from my father and brothers becomes oppressive.

I wander around the dining room to greet and talk to people. I pass my cousins, Dorian, Casim, and Salvatore.

They mingle in the crowd, but they keep an eye on the security situation, too. Everyone does. My cousins and brothers all work together to manage our security as closely as they can. I just wish they could eliminate the risk completely.

Nothing will ever eliminate the risk completely. We'll always live in the shadow of danger.

A bell rings somewhere and we all move toward the long, elaborate dining table set with expensive china, crystal wine glasses, and silver cutlery.

My father and mother take their places at the head of the table. My brothers, sister, cousins, and aunt get scattered amongst the other guests.

I find my place card and sit down next to Ambassador LeGot. At least I'll have someone to talk to tonight.

The waiters, servers, and butlers move in and start offering and pouring wine, port, and champagne for the guests. I select a Gewürztraminer. I don't know what we're having for dinner, but I can always get something else once the waiters start serving the meal.

Ambassador LeGot turns to me. "It was such a tragedy to hear about your uncle, Your Highness. My deepest condolences."

"Yes, thank you. It was a shock, especially for my father."

"It was so good of him to take your cousins into his house. I'm sure they're very grateful."

"They're like family now. Casim and Salvatore work side by side with my brothers and Dorian. We all treat them as our own, now that they have no one else."

"I'm surprised the Crown Prince hasn't tried to marry them off," he adds.

I jolt upright and spin around to stare at him. "What do you mean?"

He sips his wine. "They're old enough, aren't they? Aren't they the same age as Christophe and your brother César ? Christophe is married and.....who knows what César is doing."

I look away. I don't want to talk about César.

My family doesn't talk about César after he got accused of murder, robbing the Treasury, and went on the run from every international law enforcement agency in the world.

I should consider it inexcusably rude for some French ambassador to make a comment like that to one of the Royal Family.

I can only assume the ambassador doesn't understand why César is such a touchy subject. Maybe the ambassador thinks he's making polite conversation about something everyone already knows.

I take a sip of my wine to cover up my embarrassment, but it's too late. I already feel my cheeks flushing.

He doesn't notice my reaction, and at that moment, one of the handsome young men who was just greeting me so politely a few minutes ago leaps to his feet.

He does it so fast that he knocks his chair over flat on the floor behind him. Screams echo through the dining room when he pulls two machine guns from under his tux. The security team should have searched everyone before they let this man into the room.

He swivels his guns around, takes aim at my parents at the end of the table, and opens fire. My father and mother dive out of their chairs and take refuge under the table. So does everyone else.

I do the same thing, but the gunman is already stalking around the table to get a clear shot at my parents. They're totally unprotected over there.

The gunman passes me and I see silver duct tape stuck to the stocks and barrels of both weapons. That's the moment when I realize the truth.

He didn't pull them from under his tux. They must have been duct-taped under the table. That's how he got past the security search. The guns were already inside the room. Someone else must have planted them here.

He makes it halfway to the end of the table before Pascal leaps out of nowhere. Everyone always ignores him, but he's as sturdy and determined as all the other men in my family.

He shoots to his feet on that side of the table, pulls two semi-automatic pistols from under his jacket, and opens fire right into the gunman's chest.

The gunman staggers, but he doesn't fall. The shots tear his shirt to reveal a bulletproof vest underneath. Pascal sees them and shoots the guy in the head.

His body topples over backward and slams down on the floor right next to me. I'm still staring at it in shock when a bunch of our security guards grab me, pull me out from under the table, and practically carry me out of the hall.

They rush me out of the building and shove me in a limo with Dorian, Johanne, Marguerite, Christophe, and Geneviève. The limo squeals away and burns rubber all the way back to the Royal Palace.

We all stumble inside. Christophe hustles us into one of the palace drawing rooms where we all stand around shaking in terror—all except Christophe and Dorian.

They're both armed and holding their weapons ready for anything. Christophe pulls out his phone and makes a quick phone call.

"They identified the shooter," he tells us when he hangs up.

"Please tell me he wasn't working for my family," Geneviève quavers. "I can't go through all of that again!"

"No, he wasn't. He belongs to a random anti-monarchy fringe group. He has no connection to your family."

She covers her face with both hands and collapses on one of the couches. "Oh, thank God!"

"Someone taped those guns under the table!" I hear myself talking way too loudly. "They duct-taped the guns under the table! Someone planted the guns inside the room before we ever got there!"

"The security team is looking into that right now. They're finger-printing the guns, but we still might not be able to find the people who did this. We just have to deal with it."

"Deal with it how?" Dorian counters. "We can't stay locked up in the palace forever. We will have to go out in public for official functions. Then the same thing might happen again."

"I'll tell you what we're going to do," Christophe replies. "We're going to hire a real security expert to take over. We can't do it anymore. We need someone to take charge of our security team—someone who actually knows what they're doing."

Chapter 2: Alexei

I stop in front of the Royal Prince's Palace in Monaco and raise my hands above my head. I stare into space and wait while the security guard pats me down.

He inevitably finds the two sidearms I carry in my shoulder holsters. "I'm sorry, Sir," he tells me. "I have to confiscate these for the duration of your visit. I'll return them when you come out."

"No problem. You're doing a good job."

"Thank you, Sir." He pulls both guns from their holsters and takes them inside the security checkpoint near the palace entrance.

Then he checks his computer. "Alexei Asatiani?" he asks.

"Yes." Don't ask me why he asked me that when he just saw the name on my European Firearms Pass.

He makes another detailed inspection of the page on his screen before he says, "You can go in now, Sir. Thank you for your cooperation."

I reply, "You're welcome," and pass the checkpoint to enter the palace.

A different man greets me at the entrance. He's an older guy with short, greying hair, a long, bony face, and a long, bony body that doesn't look right in his suit.

His gaunt, haggard, deeply lined face makes his neatly trimmed goatee look scraggly even though it isn't.

He offers me his hand. "Welcome to the Prince's Palace, Mr. Asatiani. My name is Daniel Chevalier, but everyone in the palace calls me Chevalier. It's a pleasure to meet you."

I shake his hand. "Likewise. Are you the prince's bodyguard or something?"

He laughs. His eyes twinkle and his lined cheeks dimple. He has a nice smile. He looks like a good guy. He's too frail to be anyone's bodyguard. He looks like he can barely tie his shoes.

"It's good you have a sense of humor," he tells me. "That will take you far here. No, I'm the public relations manager for the whole Royal Family. It's my job to keep track of all their movements, appointments, obligations, appearances, and the like—so I'm sure you and I will be seeing plenty of each other."

"Maybe. I haven't gotten the job yet."

He skewers me with a hard look and says, "You will."

That look wipes out any idea I might have that the guy is too frail to take care of himself. He looks straight through me like he's seen it all and lived to tell the tale.

He leads me into the palace and we start walking down a long corridor.

"So....I'm not meeting the Crown Prince, am I?" I ask on the way.

"I'm afraid not. You're meeting with Prince Christophe, the Crown Prince's son and heir apparent."

I hear what Chevalier doesn't say. I know a lot about the Royal Family of Monaco—especially since I started researching this job.

Christophe might be the Crown Prince's heir apparent, but Christophe isn't his father's oldest son. The oldest, César, went on the run from justice and has never been seen or heard from since.

Christophe has a reputation for being reliable, commanding, and controlled. He must be if he's in line to take his father's throne.

The Royal Family has suffered numerous recent security incidents, some much more severe than others.

Chevalier is too polite to mention any of these. He leads me down a big, ornate corridor, up a set of small, unassuming stairs, and into an office.

It isn't the big fancy office I would expect to belong to any kind of royalty. It looks like the most ordinary, mundane, no-frills office I've ever seen. It doesn't even have a single picture on the bare, stark white walls.

A young man of about thirty-three sits behind the desk. I recognize Christophe instantly. He has dark hair, dark eyes, and a hard, set, determined look.

His eyes shoot up when I walk in and he looks straight through me, too. I didn't expect that from a prince. These people are full of surprises.

His eyes go hard and so do all the rest of his features. He gets to his feet.

Chevalier bows slightly from the waist and waves between us. "Prince Christophe, Alexei Asatiani for your ten o'clock appointment."

"Thank you, Chevalier," Christophe replies. "You can go."

Christophe remains standing and stares at me with the same direct, measuring gaze until Chevalier leaves. He shuts the door behind him. Then Christophe sits down, but he doesn't take his eyes off me.

"Thank you for coming in to see me," he begins.

I dip my chin once. "It's my privilege, Your Highness."

"Are you aware of our security situation? I'm sure you must have seen press reports of the many attacks against my family."

I nod again. "I am aware of them, Your Highness."

He rotates his chair very slightly to the left, but he doesn't take his eyes off me. "Your credentials are truly impressive. I was surprised to get someone as qualified as you."

"I do my best, Your Highness."

"Give me your assessment of our security measures—whatever you saw on your way in here just now. Tell me how you would change them if you were in charge of our security."

I hesitate.

He notices my reaction instantly. "Why do you hesitate? Is it that bad?"

I open my mouth and stop myself. "I don't want to offend you, Your Highness. I'm sure whoever has been running your security before now has been doing a stellar job."

He bursts out laughing. "That's very funny. You won't offend me because I have been running our security before now."

My eyes snap to his face. I do my best not to gasp out in shock. "You?!"

His eyes twinkle, too. He actually has a kind face when he isn't being a wall of granite to face the world. "Now do you understand why we wanted to bring in someone more qualified? Believe me. No one understands our security failings more than I do. My wife almost lost her life several times under my watch—and now we've just suffered another near-fatal attack by a deranged gunman who wants to end the monarchy. We have to overhaul our security system and I can't do that when I'm so close to the problem. Now tell me what you saw and I forbid you to spare my feelings. Tell the truth. I order you to offend me."

His eyes twinkle again when he says it and he bites back a grin. He can't order me to do anything because I don't work for him—not yet.

I probably won't ever work for him because I will offend him if I tell him.

"Well?" he demands. "Aren't you going to say anything?"

I shut my mouth with difficulty and make up my mind. I stick my hand under my jacket and pull the gun I wear in a cross-draw holster across the back of my belt.

I swing it around and his smile evaporates when I aim the weapon at his head. "This is what I think of your security system," I tell him. "If I was anyone else, you would be dead right now and I would be on my way down that hall to slaughter your entire family."

His eyes go cold and hard. "You can put the gun away, Mr. Asatiani. You made your point."

"Not quite." I holster that gun, stick my foot on the desk, and pull up my pant leg to show the other gun holstered at my ankle. Then I do the same thing with my other leg.

"The guard at the checkpoint should have searched you," Christophe snarls.

"He did. He stopped when he took my shoulder guns." I spread my jacket to show both empty holsters. "He didn't finish the search—and he stood with his back to me for almost five minutes while he checked his computer. Your security system is severely lacking. Heaven only knows what other vulnerabilities I'll find."

He compresses his lips in the first show of annoyance and he finally takes his eyes off me to check the tablet in front of him.

"You've worked in security for a long time," he goes on. "You have a dizzying amount of experience guarding some of the most powerful and influential people on the planet."

"Yes, Your Highness." I don't say anything else. I already know what's coming next.

He turns his tablet around and holds it up for me to see. "This is security camera footage from your last assignment. You were guarding Ibrahim Valiyev, the Uzbek premier, on his way to a Eurasian summit in Moscow. He was gunned down by a splinter terrorist group on the very steps leading to the venue. The shooter also killed three members of Valiyev's immediate family whom you were also supposed to be guarding."

I lock my eyes on a spot behind his head so I don't see the footage. I don't have to see it. I was there.

"Do you have anything to say about this incident in light of your obligation to protect these people?" he asks. "I wouldn't want the same thing to happen to me, my father, or the rest of my family. I'm sure you can understand."

I clamp my jaws shut so I don't lose my temper completely. I knew this was coming, but nothing prepared me to actually face it.

"I'm waiting for an answer, Mr. Asatiani," he murmurs. "I'm sure you can understand why I can't hire you until we clarify this matter."

"If it happened to you, your father, or the rest of your family would be entirely up to you, Your Highness," I snarl through gritted teeth.

"How could it be up to me when you would be the one in charge of our security? It would be your job to prevent a situation exactly like this."

He turns his tablet around before I can answer. He switches to a different piece of footage. I don't have to look at that one, either.

"The footage shows you going down shooting. You got shot five times in the chest before you collapsed. The attackers only killed the targets after you went down. The reports say you've been in the hospital for the last six months. This will be your first job since it happened."

"Yes, Your Highness," I growl. "That is all true."

"Then I would have to question your mental state when returning to the job. How do you answer that?"

"Only that I'm certain I can do the job to the Royal Family's satisfaction, Your Highness."

"How can you give me that assurance in light of this incident? How did the splinter group get near the venue if your defenses were so good?"

I lose my temper just for a split second. "Valiyev caused his own death—and nearly got me killed!"

I shut my mouth in a hurry, but it's too late. I let it slip out after I promised myself I would take that information to my grave.

He raises his eyebrows. "Valiyev caused his own death?! How?"

I've already let it out. I might as well explain it.

I can't stand the way he's looking at me, so I stare at the spot on the wall behind him. "He overruled my decisions and refused to let me implement defensive strategies I knew he needed. He cut his security budget and even released personnel I brought in to bolster security. My team and I acquired advanced intelligence of the attack, but he got this lunatic idea to make himself a martyr. He cut our defenses even more the night before the attack and he refused to wear a bulletproof vest—almost as if he knew he would die and he wanted to. More than a dozen of my people died in the attack along with Valiyev's party."

He sinks back in his seat and swivels his chair to look away from me. "That is a very serious accusation."

"I have never told anyone before. I vowed never to tell anyone." I hear my voice trembling. I choke on the words. "It was hard enough to recover from the gunshot wounds. I wasn't sure if I would even survive—and then I doubted if anyone would take me on again. I wouldn't blame you if you didn't. No one would believe me anyway."

"I believe you," he murmurs under his breath.

"Just tell me right now if you plan to do the same thing here," I blurt out. "I won't take the job if you do. If I see you or anyone else weakening the Royal Family's security or defenses in any way, I'm out. I won't go through that again."

He swivels his chair around to confront me. He looks up and his eyes drill me to the core. I realize in that moment that I'm looking back at him like an equal—and I forget to call him, *Your Highness*.

He's just a man—a human man who can die if he gets shot. Everyone in his family can die if they get shot. No one understands that better than I do.

I don't look away. I won't take the job if he thinks this is all a game he can play with people's lives—including mine. I didn't spend the last six months learning how to breathe again so someone could put me through it all a second time.

"I can assure you, Mr. Asatiani. I will spare no resource to protect my family. That's why you're here—because my brothers, my security team, and I can't protect the family on our own. If you see, hear, or find out anything that threatens my family, I want to hear about it right away, even if you think it's something that would offend me. I especially want to hear if some security measure I've implemented is lacking. That's exactly the information I'm hiring you to give me."

I look up at the spot on the wall. "Yes, Your Highness," I mumble. "That's my job."

He checks his tablet, but he does it in a way that tells me he already knows everything on it. "The rest of your record, your abilities, and your professionalism are unparalleled."

I don't answer. I don't need this man to tell me what my record, abilities, and professionalism are. My last job makes all of that irrelevant.

"I'm hiring you as my sister Simone's personal bodyguard," he goes on. "She has an extensive social and public appearances schedule. Her public profile is extremely important to the Royal Family's public relations image as being connected to and part of the younger modern generation. She's considered a culture and fashion icon, so it's extremely difficult to cut back her schedule."

"Of course, Your Highness. I understand perfectly."

"You might also like to know that she's extremely strong-willed. She doesn't take kindly to anyone telling her what to do. She doesn't want a bodyguard at all. She will resist your orders and decisions, but I'm empowering you to overrule her and even forbid her to leave the palace unless she follows your instructions."

My eyes snap back to his face. Is he really saying this? I find it hard to believe.

"I can't hire you for both positions—both as her bodyguard and as our new security chief. Her public image is more important right now and I don't have anyone nearly qualified enough to assign to her. That's why I'm assigning you. You'll work closely with our team, so you'll be able to see and understand our entire security position anyway. You can give us your assessment and recommendations. Then we'll implement them as best we can—but at the moment, you're our most qualified candidate. I want to take you on. I just have to assign you where you're most needed. I would be leaving Simone completely unguarded if I kept you back to oversee the palace. I just can't do that right now."

I look away. "I understand, Your Highness. I will do the job to the best of my ability."

"I'm certain you will, but take my warning about Simone. Her social calendar is our biggest security challenge. She moves around a lot, visits a lot of different locations, and she always interacts with her fans who follow her everywhere. You'll need to deal with all of that—not to mention her personality."

"Of course, Your Highness. I'm certain I will be able to handle it. I have guarded other clients like that in the past."

"I doubt you've guarded anyone like Simone before." He stands up. "Come with me. I'll explain the situation to her in private before I introduce you."

Chapter 3: Simone

"Why can't you just tell him move the flower arrangements out of the way?" I ask. "Why does some low-level mall manager get to decide the aesthetic of one of my appearances?"

"That's exactly what we're trying to straighten out, darling," Antoinette Dufrene tells me. "It won't interfere with the event in any case, so it isn't something you need to be concerned about. Just show up and blast your glowing charm at everyone. None of your fans care about anything else."

"They'll care if they can't even see me because some giant flower arrangement is in the way and blocking me from view." I glance at my nails. The palace nail technician sits in my apartment giving me a manicure. "When am I going to see Lucille to get dressed?"

"Chevalier has you scheduled for an eleven o'clock wardrobe appointment. You're scheduled to leave here at one and arrive at the mall at two."

I nod and then point at my nails. "Don't forget to round off the corners. They were too square last time."

The nail technician bends over her work and mumbles, "Yes, Your Highness." She's a new person. I don't even know her name yet.

Antoinette starts to say, "What did you think of the....?" when someone knocks on my apartment door.

I yell, "Come in!"

My brother Christophe strolls in and nods at Antoinette. "How is everything going?" he asks.

"Just fine," I reply over my shoulder.

He glances at Antoinette and the nail technician. "Would you two mind giving us a minute alone?"

I cringe when Antoinette and the nail technician make a speedy exit. It's never a good sign when Christophe wants to speak to me alone.

I stand up and walk over to the couch while I wait for them to leave. "What's so important?" I ask as soon as the door shuts. "I need to finish my manicure so I'm ready for my scheduled appearance later today."

"I'm hiring a bodyguard for you, Simone," he tells me. "Your heavy appearance schedule and your public profile are just too dangerous for you to continue without a bodyguard."

I groan and roll my eyes to heaven. "Not this again! We've already talked about this. I don't need a bodyguard. My fans come to see me because they love me. I've been standing in the middle of crowds of thousands of fans and none of them has ever threatened me."

"There's a first time for everything. We can't keep taking these risks without at least trying to minimize them. The man I'm assigning will be responsible for everything related to your security. He'll have the authority to dictate every aspect of your security including what you wear, when and how you arrive and leave each appearance, and everything related to the venue itself. I'm empowering him to intervene if he sees anything dangerous or even anything that could be improved when it comes to your security."

I narrow my eyes at him. I can only snarl through bared teeth. "You can't do this!"

"I'm already doing it because I already hired the guy. I'm even giving him the power to stop you from leaving the palace, so you better learn to cooperate with him if you plan to keep up your current schedule."

I shoot off the couch and forget all about keeping my voice calm. "This is outrageous! You know how important my schedule is! How am I supposed to keep up with my fan base if I don't leave the palace!"

He only shrugs. "You can leave the palace all you want as long as you cooperate with his security measures. That's all you have to do. I don't see what's so hard about that considering how many times people have tried to assassinate us recently."

"Part of my public image is that I get up close and personal with my fans! They all want to come up to me, give me things, talk to me, and get autographs and pictures! What am I supposed to do about that? All the benefit our family gets from my profile will go up in smoke if I don't keep doing it. The fans will see me hiding behind a bunch of musclemen who are there to keep everyone away from me."

"Just remember one thing. We won't need a public profile if we're dead. All of that goodwill you have with your fans won't mean anything if even one of them gets the idea to take a shot at you. You're going to accept this bodyguard whether you like it or not. We aren't here to debate it. I already hired him."

I glare at him with steam billowing out of my ears. "I really hate you, you know that, Christophe?"

"Well, I love you and I don't want to see you or anyone else in the family get killed. Some lunatic could easily use your adoring fans to get way too close to you and try exactly the same thing that happened at dinner the other night. You have to do everything this man tells you to do or it will be too dangerous for you to go out at all."

I groan in exasperation, turn away, and cross my arms over my chest while I stare out at the grounds. This is the worst yet.

I've always been able to talk Christophe out of assigning me a bodyguard. This is the last thing in the world I need—now or ever.

"I'm going to bring him in to introduce you to him," he goes on. "You'll be working closely with him from now on, so make sure you understand and cooperate with all of his decisions. Is that clear, Simone?"

I don't turn around or answer him. I won't cooperate with some gorilla who wants to cramp my social schedule. I definitely won't let some hired thug tell me when I can and can't leave the palace. I won't let anyone keep me here as a prisoner.

I don't see Christophe's reaction to my non-answer. He can get very stubborn and determined when he makes up his mind about something.

I get it that he's been responsible for the Royal Family's security for so long. He blames himself for all the breaches, attacks, and incidents that put our family in danger, especially the incidents and attacks related to his marriage to Geneviève.

I can't fault him for trying to increase security, but he doesn't have to ruin my life while he's at it.

He walks back to the apartment door, opens it, and I hear his footsteps coming back along with one other set of footsteps.

"Simone, this is Alexei Asatiani," Christophe tells me. "He'll be your new bodyguard."

I would like to stand here with my back to both of them to show them both what I think about this whole situation.

The cutting tone in Christophe's voice tells me I don't have a choice. He won't budge on this and he really does have the power to stop me from going out.

He would only have to give the word. None of the limo drivers or anyone else who works for the Royal Family would take me anywhere if he told them not to.

I turn around. The man standing next to Christophe is five inches taller, much bigger in the shoulders, and he has a hard, chiseled, square-cut facial structure that makes him look even bigger.

He wears his pale, straw-brown hair clipped in a short military style. His sharp blue eyes flash with icy fire when he looks straight at me.

He wears an impressively tailored Tom Ford navy suit with a cream-white pocket square and cuff links, but he doesn't wear a tie. He leaves his shirt collar unbuttoned, but that somehow only makes him look even more impressive and professional.

I definitely didn't imagine someone like this when Christophe said he was assigning me a bodyguard. I thought he would bring in someone like our other security guards.

Alexei certainly looks the part, but his face and eyes tell a different story. He looks more like a business executive or maybe even a head of state instead of someone who would work for a head of state.

The way he's looking at me tells me loud and clear that he will definitely use the authority Christophe is giving him. Alexei sees that right off the bat. He won't back down if he wants to stop me from going out.

Knowing that makes me hate him with a passion. He's my enemy. He's the one who will ruin my life and keep me locked up in the palace. How am I supposed to deal with this bulldozer?

He dips his chin at me once. His mouth says, "It's a privilege to serve the Royal Family, Your Highness."

"Well, it isn't a privilege for me that you're here to serve the Royal Family," I fire back. "I don't want you around. Did my brother tell you that? I don't want a bodyguard and I don't need one. You aren't welcome here. Did he tell you that?"

"Yes, he told me, Your Highness. I'll do my best to keep myself and my team as onobtrusive as possible."

I snort at him. "Something tells me you won't."

I turn my back on him and Christophe before the conversation gets any worse—if I can even call it a conversation.

Now what am I supposed to do? I would really like to ditch the guy. I won't be able to do that in the palace, but maybe I'll be able to when we get out in public.

A lot of fans usually crowd around me. Alexei won't be able to stay near me all the time. He'll have to go check on the security situation elsewhere at least some of the time. I'll be able to ditch him then.

No one will know I'm ditching him. I'll maneuver myself away from him and make it look like I got swept along with the crowd. No one will be able to argue with that.

Christophe turns to Alexei after I turn away. "Simone has a social engagement later today. She's presiding over a fashion expo at a mall downtown. That will be your first assignment. She's scheduled to meet with our wardrobe mistress at eleven o'clock. She'll leave the palace at one and arrive at the venue at two. Why don't you come down to the security office? I can go over some of the arrangements now so you'll be able to work out the best way to enter and exit the venue. Once you come back from her appearance, I want you to attend a meeting with the rest of the security team. We'll go over our wider strategy and you can make any recommendations you have."

Alexei says, "Of course, Your Highness," and they both leave without another word to me.

I collapse into the nearest armchair and cover my eyes with a groan. I have to figure out a way to outmaneuver Alexei. I can't let him interfere with my life—and my social schedule is my life.

I would go crazy without social interaction. I wasn't built for isolation—which is what will happen if I don't cooperate with him.

Now I'm saddled with this guy and everyone is going to get the wrong idea when I show up in public with him. What a nightmare this is turning out to be.

Chapter 4: Alexei

I walk into the wardrobe fitting room in the Royal Palace and look around. An older lady bustles around in there checking a million outfits hanging on a clothes rail and opening and closing shoe boxes.

She stops what she's doing to stare at me. "What are you doing in here?" she demands. "This is a private suite reserved for the Royal Family."

"I'm aware of that, Ma'am," I tell her. "My name is Alexei Asatiani. I'm Princess Simone's bodyguard. Prince Christophe just hired me this morning, so I'm here to assess the security situation before Princess Simone comes to see you in...." I check my watch. "Fifteen minutes. Could you please show me the outfit you plan for her to wear today?"

The woman's face goes through a series of different expressions from consternation to annoyance to surprise. She finally humphs under her breath and turns back to the clothes rail.

"I never heard of any bodyguard coming in here and inspecting someone's outfit before an event," she mutters.

"Then the Royal Family must not have had very good bodyguards. Prince Christophe has given me the authority to make decisions on everything related to Prince Simone's security. Please show me the outfit and kindly do it before she has to actually put it on. We don't have a lot of time."

She humphs again, takes a grey, houndstooth pencil skirt off the rail, and hands it to me. I take it, turn it around, and hand it back. "This can't be all she's wearing. What else is she wearing?"

The woman snorts at me and takes down a white blouse with a wide pointed collar and a tan blazer also with big, pointy, flared lapels.

"Do you want to inspect her shoes, too?" the woman sneers.

"Yes, Ma'am. That would be great—and her handbag and jewelry."

The woman makes a face and starts to turn away. I pretend not to notice her attitude while I take a look at the jacket and blouse.

I'm just getting ready to tell the woman what I think when Princess Simone walks into the room. She starts to say, "Did you find that pink dress I asked you about, Lucille....?"

Simone stops in her tracks when she sees me standing there with her clothes in my hand. She's five-foot-six with a statuesque figure, wavy blonde hair, and bright blue-green eyes.

I've rarely seen a woman as stunningly beautiful as she is—and she knows it. She knows she's a culture and fashion icon. That's why public appearances are so important to her.

"What are you doing in here?" she snarls.

"I'm assessing your wardrobe for today's appearance."

"You have no right to be in here!" she snaps. "This area is private."

I have to try not to groan. "Please, Your Highness. I was standing outside your apartment when your brother told you about me. He specifically mentioned that he was giving me the authority to make decisions on what you wear. How would I do that if I didn't come in here and see what you planned to wear to each of your appearances?"

I turn around and address the woman. I guess her name is Lucille.

I hold out the blazer Simone plans to wear today. "I would like you to sew a layer of Kevlar reinforcing fabric and panel plates inside this jacket—both to the two front panels and to the back....."

Simone rushes around me and slaps the jacket out of my hand. She may have been trying to grab it away from me, but she knocks the hanger out of my grasp and it hits the floor.

"You can't do this!" she snaps. "You are not going to come in here and start altering my clothes mere minutes before I'm about to leave for a public appearance?"

I don't take the bait. I bend over and pick up the jacket. "I'm sure your wardrobe mistress makes alterations to your wardrobe mere minutes before you leave for public appearances. I'm sure she does it all the time. She can do it today. Don't worry. No one will ever know the fabric is there." I hold out the jacket to Lucille. "Please add the fabric before Princess Simone leaves."

Lucille glances at Simone. Lucille doesn't take the jacket.

I gasp in exasperation and hold the jacket out farther. "Princess Simone won't be going to this appearance at all if you don't add it. I'm the one who makes that decision, not her. Now add it and don't make me say it again."

Lucille lowers her eyes, takes the jacket, and walks away from me to a doorway leading to another part of the fitting room.

Simone huffs and storms off somewhere else. I follow her.

This is all growing pains in the early stages of starting a new job. Some clients always bristle when their bodyguards try to tell them what to do.

All of these people will get used to my presence. They'll understand they can't push me around. They'll figure out that it's my job to tell them what to do. I'm not ordering everyone around because I enjoy it.

Simone enters the makeup room and throws herself in the chair in front of all the lighted mirrors. The makeup artist moves in and starts pinning Simone's hair back out of her face.

She isn't the first female client I've guarded, but she's definitely the one with the biggest attitude.

She snorts again when I go over to the makeup artist's box, take out one of the jars of concealer, unscrew the lid, and smell it.

"You don't actually think someone would poison my makeup, do you?" she chides.

"Wouldn't you rather I found out about it beforehand if they did—before someone actually put it on your face?" I put the concealer back. The makeup artist gives me a side look when I unscrew one of the lipstick tubes and smell that, too.

"What are you—a scientist?" Simone snaps.

I don't answer at all. I move over to the mountain of hair products standing off to one side. I'm studying the ingredient list of one of the hairspray cans when the hair stylist comes in to arrange Simone's hair.

The stylist takes one look at me spraying the hair spray into the air and then smelling the fumes. I don't smell anything dangerous in there.

The stylist stands off to one side waiting for me to leave. "Ignore him," Simone tells the woman. "Just do your job and pretend he isn't here. That's what I'm doing."

She isn't pretending very well. I can see her getting more and more agitated the longer this goes on.

I satisfy myself that the hair and makeup people are doing what they're supposed to do, so I go check on Lucille's progress. She sits at the sewing machine running Simone's jacket under the needle.

I see Lucille carrying out my instructions, so I don't interrupt. I check out the shoes and handbag she's set out for Simone's appearance today. Then I go back to the other room while I wait for the stylists to finish her hair and makeup.

I wait around until she returns to the wardrobe room. We walk in just as Lucille comes in with the jacket. I take it from her and inspect the fabric. She stitched in the extra panel plates between the fabric, too. The jacket isn't perfect, but it's much more protective like this.

"Everything looks good," I tell Simone. "It will fit under your jacket. No one will ever know you're wearing it."

She spins around, bellows at me, and lashes out to tear the jacket out of my hands. She misses and winds up tossing it onto the floor instead. "I'm not going to change my wardrobe for some stupid security nonsense!"

I just shrug. "You have to abide by all my security recommendations. You can take it up with Prince Christophe if you don't like it, but I could just as easily tell him that you won't take what I consider reasonable precautions. Then he'll cancel your appearance altogether. Is that what you want?"

She stands there fuming at me. She's actually really beautiful even like this. Her eyes glitter with fury and color flushes her cheeks.

I realize in this moment that Christophe was telling the truth. I've never dealt with a client as strong-willed as she is. I mean, I've dealt with plenty of strong-willed clients before, but never one so resistant to their own security measures.

She's going to be a challenge for me. I have to handle her correctly. Her security needs are exceptional. If she resists too much, Christophe might remove me and bring in someone she can actually get along with.

That would be catastrophic because she might be able to railroad the person into slacking off on her security.

I bend over, pick up the jacket, and hold it out to her. "You better get dressed. You don't want to be late."

She huffs again, snatches it out of my hand, and storms around me to rip the rest of her outfit off the rail. She snarls over her shoulder at me with her back turned. "Are you going to come into the dressing room with me, too?"

I laugh. "Only if you want me to."

She glares at me, stalks past me, and goes into the dressing room. Her voice drifts through the door to me from inside. "You already ruined today's appearance. Now I'll be showing up to the venue in a bad mood. I hope you're happy."

"You wouldn't have to show up in a bad mood if you just cooperate. I'm doing this for your safety, not to upset you."

She doesn't answer. She comes out of the dressing room wearing the outfit, glares at me again, and walks around me to the mirrors on the other side of the room.

I watch Lucille move in and adjust the jacket around Simone's shoulders. The Kevlar reinforcing layers don't show at all. No one can see that she's wearing the equivalent of a bulletproof vest under her clothes.

She gets even more annoyed and flustered when she sees me checking out her shoes, handbag, and when I watch Lucille arrange Simone's blouse under the jacket to make her look as good as possible.

Her hair and makeup complete the picture. She looks like a stunning, modern, elegant princess.

She steps into her high-heeled shoes and turns sideways to check herself out from behind. She looks fantastic. Her skirt and tightly tailored blazer accentuate her curves.

She finally turns around and narrows her eyes at me in deadly fury. "Well?" she demands. "Are we going or not?"

I wave toward the door and open it for her to leave. She struts past me and picks up speed to leave me behind.

I pick up the pace to follow her. I can see I'm going to have my hands full with her.

Chapter 5: Simone

I simmer in resentment all the way down the palace corridor and into the vestibule waiting room where I'll get into the limo to go to today's public appearance.

I have to fight my temper under control when Alexei follows me into the room. Now I'll never get rid of this guy.

He just had to throw me off my game by sticking his nose into every detail of my hair, makeup, and wardrobe routine. This isn't going to work if I can't find a way to make him back off.

He won't back off. No one has to send me a memo about that. He put his foot down about this whole Kevlar-reinforced jacket nonsense. This guy is going to be a massive problem for me.

He confirms it when the limo comes and he slides into the seat right behind me. He even sits next to me instead of across from me.

I stare out the window and do my best to pretend he isn't there, but his constant presence makes it impossible. He radiates a kind of solid power that broadcasts his existence to everyone around him. I might hate him, but no one can ignore this guy.

I have to do something drastic to make him back off, so I mutter under my breath, "I know about your last job. I know the people you were supposed to be guarding got killed. I don't know what you did or said to convince my brother to hire you, but he'll find out about you and dismiss you. You won't stick around long enough to interfere with my life."

"I'm glad you know about that," he replies. "Maybe you'll understand that I will never let anything like that happen again."

"You're a disgrace!" I fire back. "It's only a matter of time before everyone realizes how incompetent you are. Then I won't have to deal with you anymore."

He just gazes back at me in perfect calm. "Your brother would just hire someone else if I wasn't guarding you, so you better get used to it."

I snort at him, spin away, and go back to staring out the window, but his words sting. He's right. I'm stuck with this rotten situation. I can't get out of it, not even by getting rid of Alexei.

He doesn't say anything to break the silence on the way to the venue. Is he really going to be this exasperating all the time? How can anyone deal with a guy like this?

The limo pulls up in front of the mall where I'm making my appearance. I grab the door handle to get out of the seat, but Alexei takes hold of my arm to stop me.

"What are you doing?" I demand.

"Don't go out there yet—not until the security team gets into position."

"You are NOT going to spoil this appearance for me!"

He makes a face at me. "Do you think getting shot in the face and killed in front of all your fans would spoil this appearance for you?"

He infuriates me so much that I can't even look at him. Another guard opens the limo door from the outside just then and Alexei gets out.

I should want to go out there and greet my fans, but the conflict between me and Alexei stops me from going anywhere. I can't deal with him. I can't deal with any of this.

How did I get myself roped into this? My life and my social schedule worked just fine before he came along.

He extends his hand into the limo to help me out, but I don't take it. I step out of the car and immediately get mobbed by hundreds of fans all clamoring to surround me.

They would have surrounded me in the past. My old security detail wouldn't have stopped them. That's part of my image—that my fans can come right up to me, talk to me, shake my hand, get autographs, and take selfies with me.

The security team forms a ring around me to block all the fans from getting too close. The crush of bodies compresses the ring of guards. They have a hard time holding everyone off.

The fans stick their arms inside the ring, snap their phones, and wave leaflets and autograph books at me, but the guards don't let anyone near me.

Alexei stays inside the ring. He stands way too close to me, but the ring doesn't give us any more room for him to stand anywhere else.

I get trapped there by all the guards crowding around me. Alexei puts his arm around my back and steers me forward. Don't ask me how I can go anywhere with all these guards and fans blocking my way.

The ring acts according to Alexei's movements. The guards start forward at the same time. They create a tiny bubble of empty space at the center while we all head into the venue.

The guards escort me to the mall entrance where the mall's security team holds back another throng of fans. They all push and shove to get near me, but Alexei doesn't let me stop.

The guards split apart. We can walk faster now. He conducts me through a bunch of brightly lit displays to the mall's large central atrium. A fashion show is already in progress on the stage at the end of the mall, but I can't get anywhere near it.

The guards stand extra close to me, but they don't stop the fans from coming near me. The guards stand aside and the usual crush of bodies presses in on me.

I get lost in the rush of greeting people, signing autographs, and trying to hear their expressions of love and admiration over all the noise.

Alexei stays right next to me the whole time. He inspects each person who comes near me and even scrutinizes people I don't see.

The other guards stand around us, but they don't interfere, either. Maybe this isn't so bad. It isn't as good as it was before, but I might be able to work with this.

I get lost in the scuffle for a second until Alexei gets a call on his phone. He looks up and to both sides of the mall ceiling, moves the phone away from his mouth, and points upward to order one of the guards to go check something.

I barely catch a glimpse of more security guards swarming all over the mall, including on the upper levels.

Alexei keeps coordinating everyone behind the scenes. I'm barely aware of what he and the other security guys are doing. I can actually pretend they aren't here.

The thrill of all these adoring fans sweeps me away in the excitement. I love this. I'm in my element and interacting with so many people who love and admire me. I could do this all day.

Then comes the fashion show. I'm the guest of honor. The event organizers have set aside a special box where I sit near the judges and give my opinions on the outfits and styles displayed on the catwalk.

The press is everywhere, but the security team vanishes into the background. I don't see what Alexei is doing, but he must be staying close.

Nothing happens. Nothing ever happens at these events.

The fashion show ends and everyone goes around the mall to see all the exhibits and booths at the expo happening in different wings of the building.

Alexei and the security team materialize out of nowhere and surround me to protect me from more clamoring fans. The team stops a lot of people from coming near me so I can keep moving from booth to booth.

We get to the end of the row when a young woman charges between some of the guards. The woman gushes out some words of love and admiration before she lunges forward trying to hug me.

Alexei steps in front of me and blocks the woman with his body. She bounces off his iron bulk and falls back into the crowd.

I glare at him, but he doesn't seem to notice. The crush of more admirers makes us both pay attention to that, but I confront him once we work our way back to the main atrium.

"Why did you stop that woman from coming near me?!" I demand. "She was trying to hug me."

He compresses his lips in one small display of annoyance. "You're lucky I let you go through with this expo at all. This is a security nightmare. Any of these people could be trying to kill you."

"She was not trying to kill me! Look around you! None of these people are trying to kill me! They love me! They just want to get near me! You can't stop them from doing that!"

"I can and I will. Now you better finish talking to whoever you want to talk to. We'll be leaving soon."

I storm away from him seething with fury, but I have to cheer up when I face the fans. I got myself saddled with the single most annoying bodyguard in existence.

He sees enemies everywhere. He's paranoid and delusional if he really thinks these people are trying to kill me.

I go back to the fans, but the security team never leaves me alone. They shadow me everywhere and Alexei hovers right next to my side even as he coordinates all the other guards.

He even discusses things they found on the security cameras. He's covering the whole mall and even the surrounding streets.

He comes over to me half an hour later and tells me it's time to leave. I'm too furious to argue with him, especially here. I have to tell Christophe to get rid of this guy and give me someone more agreeable. I can't live like this.

The security team doesn't take me to the mall entrance where the limo dropped me off. They escort me through the expo and head down a side hall so I can exit out the back of the building.

We're just turning into the side hall when the same young woman comes up to us. "I love you, Princess Simone!" she blurts out and rushes forward with her arms out again.

Alexei dodges in front of me. My temper flares that he's interfering again. I try to get around him so I can accept the woman's attention.

I barely pass Alexei's shoulder when the woman pulls a gun and aims it at me. Alexei reacts just as fast, dives in front of the gun as it goes off, and the bullet smashes him in the shoulder.

The bullet rips through his jacket and a spray of blood spurts from the exit wound before the bullet slams me in the chest right next to my sternum. The impact against my jacket sends me staggering and I pitch over backward on the tile floor.

The security team mobs me, surrounds me, and drags me toward the other end of the hall. Alexei stays on his feet long enough to draw two handguns from under his jacket.

He opens fire on the woman and she jolts right and left as dozens of bullets unload into her body. Then he fires into her head and drops her before he charges after us.

Chapter 6: Alexei

I shake the fog out of my head and race down the hall toward the back of the mall. The Royal Family's limo will meet us there and take Simone and the security team back to the palace.

I keep turning around to aim my weapons behind me, but no one follows us. The lone gunwoman lies dead on the mall floor while the security alarm blares through the building.

I don't stick around to explain myself to anyone. The guards in front of me hustle Simone away. We have to get her out of the building immediately in case the woman wasn't working alone.

I'm certain she wasn't. The Royal Family has been suffering too many coordinated attacks.

Simone might be right about her fans loving her too much to attack her, but the Royal Family has its share of enemies—organized enemies. Killing one or more of them only releases other enemies to come out of the woodwork and take their places.

Simone doesn't resist this time. Is she starting to get the picture now?

The guards burst through the door and push her outside toward the limo parked in an alley behind the building. Another two limos pull in behind to make a convoy. This is the best way to hide which car she's driving in.

The guards rush outside with her only for another hail of machine gunfire to plaster the alley the minute they bring Simone outside.

She screams and dives for the pavement just as I make it to the doors.

I charge outside and see the guards hiding behind the limos trading gunfire with five armed men stalking into the alley. They rain bullets on the limos, shatter the windows, and stay shots ricochet off the alley walls.

I sprint over to Simone, cover her with my body, and pull her to her feet. "Get up!" I yell. "Get in the car—NOW!!"

She screams again when more bullets smash the window right next to us. I keep my arms around her so she doesn't falter or get lost in the confusion.

I yank the door open, shove her inside headfirst, and dive into the back with her. I slam the door and yell to the driver, "Go! Go! Go!"

He huddles down on the seat for protection from the gunshots. He sticks his head up. "What?"

"DRIVE!!" I roar. "NOW!!"

He slams his foot on the gas without sitting up all the way. The car skids out of the alley and Simone screams again when the side of the car screeches against the alley wall before he careens out onto the street.

The other two limos follow right behind us, but the gunfire doesn't stop. The driver sits up and swerves around one corner after another.

I try to see where the gunshots are coming from, but he changes direction too fast. Then I hear the thump of a chopper coming up behind us.

"Get down on the floor!" I yell to Simone and I push her down there just in case. "Don't stick your head up for anything!"

"What's happening?!" she shrieks.

I turn to look through the back window, and at that moment, the chopper releases a rocket that detonates the limo right behind us.

The shockwave hurls the car toward us and the fireball shatters the window right in front of my face. I duck, but not fast enough. Broken glass pelts me in the face and stings me through my shirt and jacket.

Simone screeches her head off and hides under her arms. "STAY DOWN!!" I roar and turn around to aim my weapon through the broken window.

The chopper dodges forward and I see a guy harnessed in the back with a rocket launcher on his shoulder. He tries to aim at our car next, but the chopper won't hold steady.

The third limo burns up behind us—and then my worst nightmare comes true when the car pulls alongside and drives abreast of us. The rear passenger window rolls down and a man sticks an automatic weapon through the window to aim straight at me.

I dive on top of Simone as bullets tear the car apart right above my head. I wrap myself around her to protect her. All the windows shatter on that side. Broken glass and metal fragments pelt all over me, but at least she's safe.

The gunfire rips forward to the driver's compartment and he jerks all over the place when the bullets hit him. The car swerves and almost drives off the road before a catastrophic boom goes off somewhere.

The car flips, hurls Simone's weight against me, and then the car smashes down onto its side.

I don't hear anything but the tinkle of falling glass shards, but I can't wait around for the attackers to come back. I scramble to sit up. "Get up!" I grab Simone. "We gotta get out of the car! Hurry! Come on!"

I try to stand up and wind up standing on the door. It's smashed against the pavement with asphalt right underneath my feet where the window should be.

Simone cowers whimpering on the floor at my feet.

I stick my head up and peer through the broken window above my head. "I don't see or hear anything out there. Come on. Get up. I'll boost you out of the car. Hurry!"

She doesn't move. She doesn't uncurl herself from down on the floor. I have to pick her up by the arms and try not to shake her to straighten her out.

She eventually stands up, but she cringes and huddles in front of me while she looks around at nothing. Her face screws up in a whimper of terrified misery.

I know exactly how she feels, but I can't do anything about that right now.

I take hold of her arms and pull her upright. "Look at me, Simone," I snap. "Look at me! Listen to me. We're gonna be all right. I'm gonna get you out of here, but you have to pull it together. Come on. I'm going to boost you through that window and you're going to climb out of the car. Understand?"

She nods, but she won't look at me. She won't even raise her head.

I can't wait anymore. The attackers could come back any second now. I wrap both my arms around her thighs, lift her off the floor, and heave her up toward the window.

She starts sobbing when she grasps the edge of the window and I propel her through it. "Climb down to the ground!" I tell her. "Get away from the car!"

She does it. She leaves the window free for me to jump up, pull myself out, and I climb down next to her.

I take two seconds to holster my weapons and look around. The car is a wreck. The driver is dead. The attackers aren't here anymore, but I hear the distant sound of a chopper somewhere. They aren't gone—not completely.

I take hold of Simone's hand and pull her off the road while I grab my phone out of my pocket and call Christophe on speed dial.

We're in a country part of town on a long stretch of highway between one place and another. I'm not even sure where we are and I damn sure won't take the time right now to find out.

I press the phone to my ear while I strike off across a nearby field.

Christophe answers. "Hello?"

"We got a problem...." I blurt out. "A massive problem!"

His tone changes instantly. "What happened? Where are you?"

"I don't know! A shooter attacked Simone at the mall. The shooter couldn't have been working alone because another group attacked us a few seconds later when we took Simone out of the building to the car. A chopper just followed us, took out one of the convoy limos, and blew up our car on the road. I don't know where the hell we are, but the cocksuckers will probably come after us. I need you to mobilize everything you have to come and get us."

"Okay, man, I'm on the way." He hesitates. "Is Simone okay?"

I glance at her. She's still whimpering in petrified misery while she stumbles along behind me. She barely keeps going. I have to keep tugging her by the hand.

"She's scared and upset, but she isn't hurt," I tell him. "I see a little house near here. We'll take shelter there. You'll be able to track my phone."

"I got it, man. Thank you."

"No problem. I'll see you soon."

We both hang up. Please Dear God let him come soon.

Chapter 7: Alexei

I struggle across the field, but I can't calm down. I draw my sidearm as soon as I stick my phone in my pocket. No one better mess with us out here. That's all I have to say.

I let go of Simone's hand and hold the house at gunpoint when we get near it. "Hey!" I yell. "Is anyone home?"

No one answers me. Simone stops walking as soon as I let go of her. Good. She'll stay there out of the way.

I inch up to the door, pound my fist on it, and then aim my gun through the window. There's no one home.

I yell out one more time before I kick in the door and drag Simone inside. I turn around, slam the door shut, and move the one table against the door to hold it closed.

Then I go from one window to another looking outside for anyone approaching or any sign of the chopper. It doesn't come.

The house is old and dusty. I can't tell if anyone lives here or not. Simone collapses on the couch hugging her arms close to her body. I barge through the house sweeping my weapon into every room.

The house consists of a tiny living room with one bedroom off the side. Another bed occupies the living room corner.

Old, threadbare patchwork quilts cover both beds along with a thick layer of dust. I don't see any footprints or finger marks in the dust on the floor or the furniture.

I go back into the living room and search the place. A counter runs along the backwall with some shelves attached to the wall to hold cups, plates, and a few bowls.

The house doesn't have running water, a sink, or power. Great. This isn't ideal, but it's better than nothing.

I start looking around for some way to shutter the windows or at least barricade them in case I need to defend this place. I eject the clips from my shoulder guns, put the empty clips in my pocket, and insert new clips from my belt so I'm ready if anything happens.

I don't want to holster my weapons, but I would have to be blind not to see the way Simone keeps glancing at me and immediately looking away. She's as scared of me as she is of the attackers.

She keeps twisting her hands together in her lap and smashing them between her knees. She can't keep still and perches on the very edge of the couch while she hunches her shoulders in racking tension.

I put my guns away and sit down in front of her. I stop myself from touching her again.

"We'll be all right here until they come and get us," I tell her as calmly as I can. "We just have to hold out for a little while. Can you do that? Will you be okay until Christophe and the others come for us?"

She tries one more time to look at me and her face screws up in despair instead. I clasp her hands and squeeze once. I wish I could do more to comfort her, but I still have to worry about the strategic situation.

I make another search of the house and find a little lean-to type shed attached to the back of the structure. A small door from the bedroom leads to the lean-to and another door opens behind the house.

That's where I find a spigot attached to the wall. That's the only water in the place.

I go inside and hunt through the kitchen. Pots, pans, and a few other articles crowd the shelves running underneath the length of the kitchen counter.

I find a crusty loaf of sourdough bread, a hunk of cheese, and a little crock of butter down there. All of them smell fresh, so someone must be living here.

Don't ask me how they can be living here without disturbing the dust, but I really don't think about it too hard. I taste the butter and then the cheese. They taste fine and the bread smells really good.

I pull a knife out of a basket of utensils, cut some slices of bread, put them on a plate, butter them, and cut some pieces of cheese before I take the whole thing over to Simone. "Here. Eat something," I tell her. "It will help you calm down."

I put the plate in front of her, take a mug outside, and fill it from the spigot before I take that inside, too.

I sit down on the couch next to her. The house doesn't have a coffee table, so I put the plate between us where she can get to it easily.

She's too agitated even to notice the food. I have to get through to her. "Hey!" I murmur and take hold of her hands. I wrap her fingers around the mug. "Drink some water. Here. Nice and easy."

I steer the mug to her mouth. Her hands are shaking too badly for her to do it herself.

I rest my other hand on her back to steady her while she takes a few gulps. She chokes on it, starts coughing, and breaks down in tears.

"That's all right," I breathe. "It's okay to be scared."

"Alexei....." she chokes and really starts crying hard.

"It's okay," I tell her. "You're okay. You made it. She didn't shoot you and we got out of the car."

"You....you saved my life...." she bawls.

"Hey! Stop it. I'm just doing my job. Come on. Drink some more water and eat some food. We won't be going anywhere for a while."

She sobs under her breath for a minute, but I can see she isn't hurt. She's just scared.

That's more than I can say for myself. My own pain is starting to catch up with me, now that the adrenaline is starting to die down.

I need to finish taking care of her before I fall over. "Take your jacket off," I tell her. "I need to check the Kevlar plates to make sure they're still strong enough to protect you."

She spins around and gapes at me. "What?!"

"Your jacket," I tell her. "Take it off and let me look at it."

She blinks at me in shock. She can barely comprehend what I'm saying.

She finally tugs the jacket off and hands it over. The woman's bullet is still lodged in the Kevlar plate over where Simone's chest would be.

I pry the bullet out and put it in my pocket. The plate has a hole in it now, but the rest of the jacket looks fine. I hand it back. "You can put it back on now. Keep it on in case you need it again, okay?"

She's too far gone to answer, but she puts the jacket back on in a trance. I have other things I need to take care of right now.

I go into the bedroom, pull back the quilt, and strip off the top sheet. I take it back to the living room where I can keep an eye on both Simone and the surrounding countryside.

She sniffs over there on the couch. I don't check to see if she's eating. She'll get hungry enough pretty soon. Then she'll eat.

I put both my weapons on the living room bed where I can look out the windows. Then I get busy filling a bowl with water and tearing the sheet into strips.

"What are you doing?" Simone croaks.

I groan and start pulling off my jacket and shoulder holster. "I didn't find any kind of first aid kit here." I wince when I move my shoulder. "I guess I'll just have to wait until I get back to the palace."

I lay my jacket aside, unbutton my shirt, and actually gasp when I pull it off. It's already saturated with blood on the left side. The rest of it doesn't look so hot, either.

I turn around, sit down on the bed—and see Simone gaping at me. I realize I probably shouldn't be taking my shirt off in front of a client, but it's too late. I won't be able to clean up these wounds with my shirt on.

Now she can see all my scars from my last job, but she said she already knew about that.

Blood slicks down my chest, side, and arm from the bullet wound in my shoulder, but at least it isn't serious. It tears through the shoulder muscle. It could have been a lot worse.

I dip one of the torn sheet rags in the bowl of water and start moping the blood away. I can't help but wince when I pull flecks of broken glass from my arms, chest, stomach, and even my face.

Bruises, scratches, and scuffs cover my arms, shoulders, and back. I guess I got more banged up than I realized.

"You got hurt!" Simone blurts out. "You got shot! I'm so sorry, Alexei! I didn't realize.....I didn't think....."

I don't look up. I go on cleaning the blood off myself and then making bandages for all these injuries.

She didn't realize she was in danger even though her brother, her security team, and I already told her she was. She witnessed I don't know how many attacks against her family, but she refused to believe someone would actually come after her.

Now she gets it—but not before I got shot—again. I really need to stop doing that.

Some might say I should go into another line of work, but this is all I've ever done. It's who I am now. I'll keep doing it until someone tells me I can't anymore.

I clamp my lips shut when I press a pad of fabric against the bullet wound and wrap the bandages around my shoulder. This isn't the most hygienic or professional field dressing, but it will do in a pinch.

She starts crying while she watches me. "Thank you, Alexei! I don't know how to thank you!"

"You don't have to thank me," I tell her. "What do you think—that I would let you get shot? Come on. It's all right. I got you away. That's the important thing."

I stand up and start pulling on my ruined shirt. I have nothing else to wear.

I squint through the window. "The sun is going down. It will probably get cold tonight. Come in here." I take her hand, pull her off the couch, and lead her into the bedroom. "You sleep in here tonight. I'll take the living room."

I push her down to lie on the bed. She doesn't resist when I cover her with the quilt and tuck her in.

I don't want to strike any kind of light or fire. Someone might see that.

"Thank you, Alexei!" she whimpers again when I rub her back.

"Go to sleep," I tell her. "I'll be watching."

I go back to the living room and find some boards in the lean-to. I use them to block out all but one window. The boards won't protect us from everything, but this is all I have to work with right now.

Chapter 8: Simone

I startle out of a sound sleep and bolt upright in bed. I look around everywhere trying to figure out where I am.

All the terror of the mall attack comes rushing back. Is someone coming after me right now?

I still feel the impact of the bullet hitting my chest. I keep reliving that sensation over and over again. I feel like I'm getting shot right now.

I would be dead now if Alexei hadn't insisted that I alter my jacket. I would also be dead now if he didn't stop in front of me and take the bullet first. His shoulder slowed it down.

I can't believe he got so hurt protecting me. I can never forgive myself for that.

I caused that. I caused him to get hurt—and I don't even know how many people got killed in that attack.

I should have listened to him and Christophe. I should have listened to the evidence of my own senses. How could I ignore so many attacks against my family? What was I thinking?

A shadow eases out of the darkness near me. I recoil when I see a shadowy figure coming toward me.

Then I recognize Alexei's voice in the darkness. He murmurs low in a soft, comforting whisper. "Hey! It's only me. Are you okay? Did something wake you up?"

I choke down despair. We're in the little country house where he brought us after the attackers destroyed the limo.

Has he been sitting up keeping watch over me to protect me even here? He said he would. Why do I doubt that?

Never in a million years would I have believed he could do all this. He got hurt covering me with his body. All those glass chips embedded in his face—he took them protecting me.

"Everything's all right," he murmurs. "No one is out there. It's all quiet. Try to go back to sleep."

He barely says the words before his phone vibrates in his pocket. He takes sit out and the screen casts an eerie greenish glow on his chiseled features.

He's still holding one of his sidearms in one hand. He's still wearing his shirt and suit jacket with all the blood stains all over them.

He's such a Terminator. He'll never stop as long as he's still alive. He would have died before he let anyone harm me.

He answers the phone and I hear Christophe's voice coming through from the other end, but I can't make out the words.

Alexei clips his words of short. "Yeah. Yeah. I got it. Yep. We're ready when you are. Yeah, I'll tell her. Thanks."

He hangs up, puts his phone away, and turns to me.

"The security team is coming in with another chopper to pick us up. They're on their way in now while it's dark. They figure now is the safest time. Come on. Get up and come into the living room. I want you to sit on the couch—and stay low when the chopper comes in just in case it all goes to shit. Understand? If the lead starts flying, you get down on the floor and hide behind the couch. Got it?"

I nod. I'm too panicked even to speak right now.

He takes hold of my arm, pulls me out of bed, and leads me into the living room. He puts me on the couch while he stands against the wall next to the window.

He's barricaded all the others. That's the only window where he can see out.

I go back to shivering and cringing on the couch. I'm not cut out for situations like this—or any kind of danger. Give me a dinner party or any kind of social event. Then I'm in my element.

He's definitely in his element here. He handles every detail of this situation so perfectly. I trust him more than I ever could have imagined. I can't believe I hated him so much when I first met him.

The plate of food he set aside for me isn't there anymore. I should have eaten it when I had the chance.

That doesn't matter because I'll get all the food I want back to the palace.

It's the thought that counts, though. He did everything to take care of me and calm me down. He did all of that before he took care of himself even though he was walking around with a gunshot wound.

I can't believe he only did that because it was his job. None of that was his job. The comfort and tenderness he's been giving me isn't his job. I don't believe that for an instant.

None of the other security guys on our team would have done that. They're all too in awe of the Royal family.

He glances over at me, and right then, we hear a chopper coming closer. He aims his weapon at the window and his phone rings again.

He answers it and holds it to his ear while he watches the chopper descend onto the field outside.

"Yeah!" he yells into the phone. "Yeah! Go ahead!"

A bunch of armed gunmen deploy from the chopper and swarm across the field toward the house. Alexei rushes over to me, puts his arm behind my back, and pulls me to the door. "Let's go!" he yells.

He has to drag the table out of the way so we can get outside. He breaks into a run and rushes me along with him in a dead sprint for the chopper.

The gunmen rotate back and forth aiming their weapons in every direction except at us. The men hold the surrounding countryside at gunpoint until more security guys pull me into the chopper.

I flop down in the seat and they buckle my harness around me. Alexei climbs in next to me and all the armed guards load up before the chopper lifts off.

Tears of relief stream down my cheeks as we climb higher and leave the little house behind. I'm safe. It's over.

Alexei squeezes my hands in my lap one more time. He doesn't do anything else, but that's enough. He sits next to me all the way back to the palace.

The chopper sets down on the roof and I lose track of Alexei when we all go inside. The medical team takes me to the palace medical clinic where I collapse on the exam table while they examine me.

Alexei doesn't come in. He needs more medical attention than I do.

"Where's Alexei?" I ask the medical team. "Is he all right?"

"I don't know where he is, Your Highness," one of the nurses tells me. "Lie still while we finish examining you. You can go back to your apartment as soon as we make sure you aren't hurt."

"I'm not hurt. You have to take care of Alexei."

"Yes, Your Highness," she tells me. "You can check on him as soon as we finish."

I have to lie down. I wish they would hurry up, but my strain and exhaustion are starting to catch up with me.

I tolerate the examination as well as I can. I'm anxious to get out of here, but I start to wilt the longer this goes on.

I've been so high strung for the last twenty-four hours since the attack. I haven't been able to relax. Now I feel myself starting to collapse even though nothing bad really happened to me.

I shut my eyes. I really need to lie down somewhere and sleep for a long time before I think about doing anything else.

Chapter 9: Alexei

I climb down from the chopper and hustle Simone inside. The medical team stands there waiting. They bundle her off somewhere to take care of her. She isn't my problem anymore.

I walk through the doors and down the stairs to enter the palace, but I don't go to the palace medical clinic. I need to, but I turn off toward the security office instead.

I only make it halfway down the hall before Christophe comes up to me from the other end. He stops in front of me and narrows his eyes at the scratches on my face. "You got hurt."

"It's nothing, Your Highness."

"Thank you....for my sister's life," he tells me.

I only nod. "That's my job, Your Highness. I told you I would protect her. What's the security situation? We should assess our threat level and make sure we have all our bases covered before we let our guard down. That's just my personal view, Your Highness—and you did say you wanted to hear my opinions on the subject."

He scrutinizes me extra closely. "I think the time has come for you to stop calling me that."

I open my mouth and stop myself.

"You saved my sister's life—and we coordinated for you to get her back safely," he goes on. "I have a feeling you're going to be working with us for a long time. You don't have to be so formal. You can call me Christophe."

I open my mouth and falter again. "I don't know if I can do that, Your Highness."

"Why not? I'm sure you have acquaintances out in the world with whom you are on a first-name basis. Don't you?"

"Yes, Your Highness, but you're not an acquaintance."

He laughs and claps me on the shoulder—the other shoulder—thank God. "We may not be now, but I hope we can become friends someday. In the meantime, I want you to call me Christophe. Will it offend you if I call you Alexei?"

"No, Your Highness."

He laughs again. "Just think about it. Come on. Let's go see what's happening." He leads the way down the hall to the security office. "We got a lead on the woman who shot you," he tells me on the way. "She and all the gunmen your team killed belonged to Blood Tide, the same splinter terrorist group that killed Valiyev."

I stop in my tracks and spin around to gape at him. "No! That's impossible!"

"Why do you say it's impossible? Blood Tide is still operational. It isn't that far from Uzbekistan to Moscow or from Moscow to here."

I struggle to put my eyes back in their sockets. "Are you saying.....are you saying....they came after me?"

"No, no. Nothing like that. My father is in negotiations with Ardavan of Tajikistan, Asanaliev of Kyrgyzstan, and Cumali of Turkmenistan—the same heads of state Valiyev was meeting at the time of his death."

I choke on the words. "What does that have to do with Simone?"

He shrugs and keeps walking. I have no choice but to follow him. "I suppose Blood Tide is trying to sabotage the diplomatic process by targeting the parties involved. Simone is just the easiest target because she has the highest public profile."

I struggle to get my voice under control. "I don't know if I can believe that."

Now he's the one who stops in the middle of the hall and turns toward me. "This never had anything to do with you. These people look for security vulnerabilities they can exploit. They did it with Valiyev and they're doing the same thing with Simone. Valiyev gave them too many opportunities—and I guess we can all admit now that Simone is doing the same thing."

"What can we do about it, though? You said you couldn't cut back her schedule because it would hurt the Royal Family's public image."

"I've changed my mind—or let's just say that the situation has escalated to the point where we can't continue to prioritize our image over security. I'm going to curtail her schedule—and don't worry. I'll be the one to tell her. You won't be anywhere nearby."

I look away. "I suppose she'll be able to hear it a little better after yesterday."

"I think so, too. Now I think you better go to your room, change your clothes, clean yourself up, and take at least the next twenty-four hours off. Simone won't be going anywhere. You need to rest."

I nod at the floor. I shouldn't even be standing up right now.

He pats me on the shoulder and uses his hand to turn me around and push me away down the hall. I drag myself back to my room in the servants' quarters. That's where I'm staying while I work here.

I collapse on my bed and shut my eyes in relief. Simone is safe and we both made it back alive. I call that a win.

Chapter 10:
Simone

I jump out of my skin when someone knocks on the door of my apartment. My hand flies to my heart and I spin around to see if someone is coming to attack me again.

"Who's there?!" I demand, but I hear my voice shaking.

"It's Christophe," he tells me from outside. "Are you all right in there?"

"I'm fine." I turn back to my dresser, but I can't stop shaking. Everything makes me jump now.

He must hear the tremor in my voice. He comes inside without waiting for me to invite him.

He comes over to the dresser and goes down on one knee next to my chair. I can't look at him, but he must be able to see how jumpy and skittish I am.

I don't know what's wrong with me, but maybe getting shot in the chest had something to do with it.

"I was so worried about you," he murmurs. "I know you were scared, but you're safe now. We're doing everything in our power to make sure that never happens again."

I try to snort at him while I fumble with the makeup and other stuff on top of my dresser. "Go on and say you told me so. You told me this was going to happen. Go on and say it."

"I wasn't going to say that. I'm just worried about you." He pauses and looks down long enough to see my hands shaking. He covers them with his hands to steady me. "It's all right. No one can get to you here."

I gulp and look away. "I can't relax. I don't know why."

"It's normal. You had a traumatic experience."

I try to snort again, but it comes out more as a groan. "Where's Alexei? Is he all right?"

"He's fine. I just saw him down the hall. We talked about the woman who shot you in the mall."

I spin around. "He isn't in the clinic?! Why didn't you send him there?"

He frowns at me. "He's fine. He didn't need to go to the clinic. He was more concerned with the security situation. He wants to make sure the situation is secure before we do anything else."

"He got shot, Christophe!" I shoot out of my chair. "You have to send him to the clinic right away! What is the matter with you?!"

His jaw drops. "He....what?"

"He got shot in the shoulder! Jesus, didn't you see his shirt all stained with blood?! He stepped in front of the gun! The bullet went through his shoulder before it hit me!" I barge past him. "Where is he? I have to see him!"

He springs to life and dodges in front of me. "Wait a minute. Are you saying he did all of this....everything at the house and everything .....the limo crash and all of it....with a gunshot wound?"

"Yes!" I roar. "Will you listen to me?! That woman pulled a gun on me and he stepped in front of her right before the gun went off! He bandaged his shoulder at the house....and he was covered in blood and bruises and gashes from broken glass from the limo wreck! Didn't you know?! Jesus, we have to find him and send him to the clinic. Come on!"

I storm out of the apartment and down the hall heading for the servants' quarters. Christophe tails me all the way.

I can't believe Alexei is walking around with his shoulder like that and he hasn't even gone to the medical clinic to get it taken care of.

"I didn't know!" Christophe murmurs on the way. "He played it off and said it was no big deal. I thought he was just exhausted."

"Of course he played it off!" I snap out the side of my mouth. "He wanted you to think he had it under control."

"Did he have it under control?"

I wheel around to confront him. "Of course he did! How can you even ask that? I can't count the number of times he saved me before we got to the house—and once we got there, he had the whole place locked down in minutes. He was amazing. No one has ever taken such good care of me."

He stares into my eyes reading more than I want him to, but I don't care. He needs to understand everything Alexei did for me.

Christophe only touches my elbow. "Come on. Let's go find him."

We enter the servant's quarters and Christophe knocks on Alexei's door. He lives in a small room down the hall from the chauffeurs.

The room is only big enough for a queen-sized bed, a dresser, a wardrobe, a desk with a lamp on it, and a chair. A fla-screen TV hangs on the wall opposite the bed. That's the whole room.

Alexei pulls the door open wearing just his pants and belt. He isn't wearing his bloody old shirt anymore.

The big sheet bandage he put on at the house still wraps around his chest and shoulder. He doesn't look as terrible now as he did then, but he still looks pretty bad.

The bruises have darkened and the swelling around all the cuts makes them look worse. The cuts on his face look puffy, too.

His eyes dart back and forth between me and Christophe. "Can I help Your Highnesses?" he asks.

"Cut it out!" Christophe fires back. "You didn't tell me you got shot at the mall!"

Alexei shrugs. "It didn't seem relevant at the time."

"Of course it's relevant!" Christophe snaps. "You should be in the medical clinic. Go down there right now! That's an order. Don't you dare hide something like this from me again!"

"I wasn't trying to hide it. I didn't get a chance to tell you before and we were more concerned with Princess Simone once we brought her back to the palace."

"You told me the blood on your shirt was no big deal!" Christophe counters. "You went through our entire conversation as if nothing was the matter."

"The security situation is more important."

"It's not more important than your health! Now go to the clinic—now!"

"As Your Highness wishes." Alexei picks up a clean grey T-shirt from the bed behind him and starts to open it so he can pull it on.

"Don't even bother!" Christophe snaps. "Just go the way you are."

Alexei walks past the two of us to leave the room. Christophe and I follow him down the hall to the clinic.

The medical team moves in and they practically go into hysterics when they realize he has a gunshot wound.

Christophe and I retreat out of the medical team's way. They start an IV in Alexei's arm, shoot him full of painkillers, and then start to anesthetize the wound site so they can suture it.

Alexei looks somehow so much bigger lying there with his shirt off. He dwarfs everyone else in the room, but he also looks more vulnerable.

Now nothing stops me from seeing just how hurt he really is. I was too worried about myself at the country house.

He groans when he lies down on the exam table. He flinches when they stick their needles into the wound site to numb the pain.

He's one of the strongest men I've ever met, but he can still hurt. The other gunshot scars on his chest prove that.

Seeing him with his shirt off like this and at the country house makes me understand so much more about him. I realize only now what he risked when he stepped in front of me to take that bullet.

Christophe pulls me out of the room, but we don't leave. We hover in the hallway doing nothing.

"I'm sorry, sweetheart, but I have to cut back your social schedule," Christophe tells me. "We're doing everything we can to get to the bottom of who's behind this, but we need to take better precautions in the future so this doesn't happen again. I hope you understand and you aren't too upset about it."

"Of course I understand. Do you think I wanted something like this to happen?" My hand flies to my head. "I can't believe I buried my head in the sand for so long! I can't believe I was so rude to him! I wouldn't have believed he could do all that, Christophe—not after the reports on his last job."

His eyes go hard. "What do you know about his last job?"

"I know his clients wound up dead along with half of Alexei's security team. The reports made it sound like he was incompetent as a security specialist."

"Did he tell you how those people died? Did he say anything to you about it?"

"No. He just said he was glad I knew so I would understand that he wouldn't let it happen again."

"His last client sabotaged Alexei's security protocols. The client undermined and dismantled Alexei's systems, cut his security budget, dismissed his personnel, and played games with his own life to deliberately weaken his security profile so he could make himself a martyr. He reduced all the security the night before the shooting. That's how it happened—and Alexei almost died in that shooting. He isn't what the reports make him out to be."

I blink at him in horror. "My God! That's awful!"

"You said he handled it at the house...."

"He handled everything. He handled the woman. He handled the shootout in the alley. He handled the limo ride. He handled the crash. He handled things at the house. He handled everything—I mean literally everything. I couldn't believe it."

He turns away. "We better get out of here. He probably won't appreciate us lurking around making a fuss over him."

He walks me back to my apartment, hugs me, and assures me that he's dealing with the security situation to get my social schedule back up and running.

I go back inside my apartment, sink down in a chair, and bury my face in my hands. How did I ever judge Alexei so wrongly? I have to find a way to make it up to him—but how?

Chapter 11: Alexei

I stretch out on my bed and try not to move my shoulder when I adjust my position. It feels a lot better since the medical team cleaned it up, sutured it, and put me on a course of antibiotics.

Working for the Royal Family is pretty good. They take good care of their people. Not many of my previous clients have taken such a close interest in their employees' wellbeing.

I extend my hand to the bedside table near me, grab the sandwich I got from the kitchen, and take a bite. I don't even sit up to eat my food. I'm on R&R here.

At least I think I am until a knock on my door makes me sit up. "Come in!" I call.

The door opens and I freeze when Simone steps across the threshold. I realize again with a stab of alarm that she's seeing me with my shirt off. She's been doing that a lot lately, but at least I'm not covered in blood now.

She glances around and then comes back to staring at me. "I....I just wanted to make sure....you know.....that you're recovering okay."

"I'm fine." I get to my feet, pull open one of my dresser drawers, and pull on a T-shirt so I'm not standing in front of her half-naked. "How are you?"

"I'm okay...." She fidgets. She doesn't look okay—not the way she was before the shooting. She still looks terrified.

That look twists in my guts. I feel for her, but something tells me this isn't just a friendly visit.

"Are you....how's your shoulder?" she asks. "Do you need anything? Is the medical team taking care of you? We could send you out to the regular hospital if you need it."

"I don't need anything. My shoulder is fine—or it will be as soon as it heals up. The medical team is great. I have no complaints."

"I just thought....you know.....after everything that happened...."

"Don't worry about it. I'm just glad you're okay and that we got you home in one piece. That's the most important thing."

She shuffles her feet and looks around again. I don't say another word. I have to be careful. I don't want her getting attached to me.

Something could happen to me. Something could happen to her. Anything could happen. The shooting proved that.

"I....uh....." she stammers. "I'm really sorry.....about everything I said...."

"Forget it," I tell her again. "It doesn't mean anything."

"It does!" She looks right up at me with eyes overflowing with hidden meaning.

A thousand confused feelings struggle and churn in those eyes. She's terrified—mostly of herself for coming here.

She's standing alone in my room—just the two of us. I see it written all over her face, but I don't react. I have to keep it professional no matter what.

She's beautiful—and now I see how tender and vulnerable she really is.

She isn't some kind of icon. She isn't really a princess. She's just a scared, vulnerable, confused young woman whose whole world is crashing down around her ears right now.

"I'm sorry....that I brought up your last job....Christophe....he told me what happened....and everything.....I'm sorry.....I know I can't take it back....and all the terrible things I said to you in the wardrobe room....I just want to say....I know what I did was wrong....and I promise I won't do it again. I'm so grateful for everything you did for me...I'm ashamed that I treated you that way."

"You don't have to be." I hear my voice shaking. I shouldn't let it, but it happens anyway.

"I promise I won't give you any more trouble. I'll cooperate with all your recommendations. I give you my word."

"Thank you," I tell her. "I appreciate that. I really only have your safety in mind."

She nods. "I realize that now.....and thank you for putting those plates in my jacket. I should have listened to you.....but I will from now on. I'll do whatever you think is best. I promise."

"Thank you," I tell her again. "I'm glad it worked out in the end."

She squirms and rushes out of the room. She forgets to shut the door.

I go sit on my bed while I finish my sandwich, but I don't want to lie around on R&R anymore. The threats are still out there. The whole Royal Family is in danger. That didn't stop when I brought Simone home.

I go down the hall to the bathroom, take a shower, comb my hair, and put on a suit before I go to the security office and check in with Christophe and the others.

I spend a few hours going over their security measures, but I can't get the problem off my mind. I spot a few holes in their systems, but not enough to explain all the incidents they've been having.

I take a walk in the grounds to try to clear my head. My last job still haunts me. I wish I could say it didn't, but it does.

I don't completely trust myself to protect the Royal Family the way I should. I know the shooting in my last job wasn't my fault and that I'm doing everything possible to protect the Royal Family.

I can't stop nagging doubts from creeping in. What if I'm missing something? What if some oversight of mine lets in the killer who wipes them all out?

I hike around the perimeter of the grounds and even look over the walls into the surrounding streets. Of course I don't find anything.

Christophe's defenses are really pretty good. I have to admit that. He isn't a professional and it shows, but he still did an amazing job considering he's one of the target clients.

I can tighten up the ship, but I can't completely eliminate the threat. That's the real problem. Someone somewhere will always want to try to make an attempt on the Royal Family—either one of them or all of them.

I'm on my way back to the palace when I spot movement coming from the left. I duck into the trees in time to see a young guy with long brown hair clamber over the outer perimeter wall.

He springs down onto the grass, darts from flowerbed to flowerbed, and creeps behind the hedges getting closer to the palace.

I sneak from one covered place to another to watch him. How did he get inside? Christophe increased security twentyfold after the recent assault—and that's nothing compared to what he'll do after the attack on Simone.

The Royal Family already had a regular rotating patrol of guards covering the whole perimeter wall.

They can't guard every square inch of the wall on the outside, but they do have the whole inside perimeter covered.

Some random joker off the street shouldn't have been able to jump that wall and get near the palace.

The guy comes to the end of the hedge. He can't go any further without stepping out into the open. He looks toward the apartments on this end of the building.

That's the moment when I realize he's right outside Simone's apartment. Christophe and his wife Geneviève live in the next apartment down from Simone's. Their younger brother Pascal lives next to Simone on the other side.

This asshole must have designs on one of the Crown Prince's daughters—or maybe the piece of shit intruder has designs on Simone specifically.

Sure enough, the idiot steps right out in front of God and everyone and heads straight for her patio doors.

She probably doesn't keep them locked. The scumbag can walk straight inside and do what he wants. He might even be able to tie her up, gag her, and assault her right there in the palace.

The thought infuriates me. I don't think so. I dart out of my hiding place, skim along behind the hedge, and rocket out to charge the guy from behind.

He sees me just in time to turn around before I tackle him down hard on the patio paving stones. He yells out when I land on top of him and tries to squirm out of my grasp.

I rear off him to strike him down, but at that moment, he swings around holding a gun in his hand. I barely have time to see it before it goes off right in my face.

Chapter 12: Simone

I snap wide alert when a gun goes off right outside my patio doors. I know that sound. It strikes terror into my heart.

I can't run and hide from it right here in the palace. I go over to the doors and peek out from behind the curtains.

I scream out when I see Alexei lying on the ground with blood all over his face. I hardly recognize him.

I don't stop screaming for help. I tear the doors open and rush outside, but there's nothing I can do. I grab him and try to lift him up, but he's unconscious and he's too big and heavy.

I turn in every direction yelling my head off for help. That's the moment when I spot some random stranger jumping over the wall and vanishing outside into the city streets.

I can't do anything about that now. A dozen security guards rush me from all over the grounds. They take one look at Alexei and get on their phones to call both the Police and an ambulance.

Someone must have called the medical team. Christophe grabs me and pulls me away so they can work on Alexei.

I can't stand seeing him hurt again. I want to cry when the medical team swarms all over him. I can't even tell what they're doing—and then the ambulance crew shows up.

They do a whole lot of terrible-looking stuff to him. They put a collar around his neck, an IV in his arm, and strap him down to a backboard before they wheel him away.

I really do start crying after he leaves. He can't be hurt again—not when I think about everything that happened at the mall and afterward.

What if one of these times he gets hurt so badly that he can't survive it? He barely survived the shooting that killed Ibrahim Valiyev.

This job is dangerous. Will the next time be Alexei's last? Was this the last time?

Christophe turns to me as soon as the ambulance crew leaves. "What happened?" he demands. "How did this happen?"

"I don't know?!" I howl. "I heard the gunshot and I came over to the window and I saw him lying here! That's all I know! Then I saw a guy jumping over the wall—over there! That's all I saw!"

Christophe casts a fierce look around. "No one should have been able to get inside the grounds."

"You can't let anything happen to Alexei, Christophe!" I start crying harder when I realize the truth. I care about Alexei. I care about him as more than just my bodyguard.

Christophe leans in close and lowers his voice. "Listen to me. He's tough, okay? He's survived worse than this and still come back for more. He's going to make it. I'm certain of it."

I want to believe that more than anything, but what if Alexei doesn't make it one of these times? What if next time is the last time?

The idea upsets me so much that I can't even think straight. Christophe takes me back inside my apartment, gives me some more assurance that he'll make sure Alexei is well taken care of, and leaves me alone in my despair.

I care about Alexei. I would give anything to get closer to him, but it will never happen. He's an employee of the Royal Family.

All the employees have to sign a contract not to fraternize or get involved with anyone from the Royal Family. The employees all have to agree to that before they come to work here.

That guy shot Alexei right outside my apartment. Was the intruder trying to break in here? He must have been. Alexei saved me again. He got shot saving me—again.

I can't live with this. I can't live with caring about someone who means so much to me who might get snatched away from me at any second.

Christophe leaves me alone in my apartment, but I can't sit still with this weighing on my mind. I wash my hands four different times trying to get Alexei's blood out from under my fingernails.

I pace around for hours, but my agitation becomes unbearable. I leave my apartment and head for the dining room or maybe the parlor. I need to talk to someone.

I find my parents, my aunt, my cousins, my brothers, Geneviève, and Emeline all standing around outside the dining room. None of them looks interested in food.

"We should have heard something from the doctors by now," Dorian remarks. "Alexei has been in the hospital for almost four hours."

"That's nothing if they had to operate on his brain," Pascal points out.

"Don't say that!" Emeline exclaims. "That's terrible!"

"He suffered a gunshot wound to the head," Salvatore reminds her. "What would they be operating on if not his brain?"

"He could be in surgery all night for all we know," my father adds. "He'll be in recovery for a long time even when he does get out."

"He probably won't return to work," Casim suggests. "What a shame. He was incredible."

"We don't know that," Christophe interjects. "We don't know how serious his injuries are."

"They looked awfully serious just now when the ambulance crew took him away," Pascal remarks.

"It wasn't like he got his head shot off," Renáld points out.

"Renáld !!" Emeline shrieks. "How can you say that?"

"What?" Renáld asks. "Okay, so he was covered in blood, but his head was still intact. He was still breathing and his heart rate was still good. We all saw that."

"I've heard enough wild speculation and conjecture," my father interrupts. "We're going down to the hospital to see him and get some answers from the doctors. Get the limos up here, Christophe. Did you contact the hospital to assign Alexei to a private room?"

"Yes, of course. He's even assigned to a separate wing so we can visit him."

"Good. Get the security team together. We're going to get some answers."

The whole family bursts into a flurry of activity. I race back to my apartment to change my clothes, meet back up with my family, and we all load into the limos to drive to the hospital.

I ride with my parents, Aunt Marguerite, and Emeline. The others spread out between the other limos.

I stare out the window on my way there. These are all the people I'm closest to in the world, but none of them knows how I feel about Alexei.

I shouldn't feel anything for Alexei, but I do. I feel a lot for him. I feel like I'm going to die if anything happens to him. I feel like the world would end if I didn't get a chance to at least tell him how I feel about him.

The limos pull up to a private entrance behind the main hospital building. The sign over the door says, *Mechanical Plant Entrance.*

The security team meets us there and ushers all of us into a private corridor. We're the only people down here apart from a few hospital maintenance people.

We get into the elevator. "Did you talk to the doctors?" my father asks one of the security guards on our way upstairs.

"Not yet, Your Highness," the guy replies. "We checked with the hospital reception desk before you and the Royal Family left the palace. Alexei was just coming out of surgery then. The doctors weren't available to give any report. I figured we should just wait until you got here."

My father nods at nothing. I guess we just have to accept that until we meet the doctors.

We ride up the elevator to the twenty-third floor where one of the hospital administrators meets us. She leads us to the private ward where we find Alexei lying unconscious on his hospital bed.

My hand flies to my mouth when I see him with a tube down his throat, another in his nose, and a million wires connected to every part of him.

A giant wad of bandages surrounds most of his head. We can barely see one of his eyes. Black bruising and heavy, puffy swelling disfigures what little we can see of his face.

The EKG machine bleeps next to him every time it registers his heartbeat. At least he's still alive. He survived the surgery.

A man's voice startles us from behind. "Your Highness?"

We all turn around and come face to face with a middle-aged male doctor with wavy grey hair, tiny glasses, and a long white lab coat over his dark grey-brown suit.

"I'm Doctor Bessette," the guy announces. "I'm the plastic surgeon who operated on Mr. Asatiani."

"Plastic surgeon!" Christophe exclaims. "He got shot in the head. Why would he need a plastic surgeon? Shouldn't a neurosurgeon have operated on him?"

The doctor smiles at him. "Mr. Asatiani did not suffer any brain damage in the attack. He must have turned his head very slightly when he saw the gun aimed at his face. The bullet deflected off his cheekbone and grazed the side of his face. It bruised the bone, but didn't break it. The bullet cut a gash through his cheek and scalp and cut part of his earlobe. I only had to repair the soft tissue damage. I'm certain he'll make a full recovery."

I wilt into a nearby chair in a puddle of relief. I cover my face and heave a shaky sigh. Alexei is going to be okay. The gunshot only scarred him. Thank Heaven.

I barely hear anything else the doctor says to my father. The doctor leaves us all alone. "We should go back to the palace," my father tells us. "We can't do anything else here except create another security problem for ourselves and everyone else.

I don't want to leave. I want to stay by Alexei's bed until he wakes up. I want to be the first person he sees when he wakes up. How did this happen? How did I get so head over heels attached to him so fast?

He saved my life—countless times. He was so impossibly kind to me at the country house. I've never known anyone like him.

I can't let him go. I don't know how, but I need this man in my life—as something so much more than a bodyguard.

Chapter 13: Alexei

I wake up and groan. My head feels ten times its normal size. I touch my face and feel bandages all over my head. At least I'm alive.

I don't feel like it, though. I feel like I got hit by a train.

My one unbandaged eye barely opens at all. The eyelids are so swollen they feel like they weigh a ton.

I look around and groan again when I see the Royal Family gathered around my bed.

The Crown Prince smiles down at me. "You gave us all a terrible scare, young man. You really can't go getting yourself hurt like this if you're going to be such a hero to us all. We can't afford to lose you."

I shut my one good eye and try to turn my head away, but I can't turn away from him. "The intruder...." I husk. "He....he was trying......to break in.....to Simone's room....."

"We captured the guy," Dorian replies. "You don't have to worry about the intruder anymore, brother."

I collapse in blessed relief. "Thank God."

"We just want you to get better," Christophe tells me. "We're all so thankful to you for saving her again—and that you're going to be all right."

"What happened....to me.....?" I gulp hard. Talking takes all my effort. I struggle even to stay awake.

"The bullet cut you across the side of the face and head," Pascal replies. "It didn't break any bones. Don't worry. You won't look as ugly as I do."

Some of the others laugh. I can't. "I thought I was going to die."

"You came close that time—again," the Crown Prince tells me. "You really must take better care. We insist on it."

"Trying to....." I feel myself drifting out of consciousness. "Had to.....save Simone......"

I must have passed out because I wake up without the bandages on my head. The room is empty. I'm alone. How long have I been in the hospital?

I can't move my head off the pillow. It throbs like crazy.

I barely manage to pick up my arm to touch my face. I trace the long line of stitches running from my cheek past my ear and into my scalp. The rest of my face just feels swollen. Thank God.

I shut my eyes just trying to stay alive. I'm going to be okay. I didn't dodge the bullet, but I survived in much better shape than I expected.

I float in and out of a hazy sleep. I come back to my senses more and more each time I wake up. Now I know I'm going to be okay.

The medical team keeps coming in to check on me. They all assure me I'm going to be fine—and now I know it's true.

I wake up on the third day—at least I assume it's the third day. I feel semi-normal. I might even think about getting out of bed today.

I hope things start to calm down at the palace. I want to get back there and check on things. I especially want to check on Simone to make sure she's okay.

She came with the rest of the family to visit me, but she didn't talk. She hung back on the edge of the group. She looked scared and upset again. I don't like seeing her like that.

The intruder could have broken into her apartment after he shot me. None of the Royal Family said he didn't.

He better not have hurt her. There is no prison strong enough to protect the guy if he did.

I'm lying there staring at the ceiling when one of the palace security guards enters my room. His name is Felix. He's a good guy.

"Hey, man," I murmur. "What are you doing here?"

"You have a visitor. Princess Simone is here to see you. She's waiting outside. We just wanted to make sure you were awake and alert enough to see her."

"Uh...yeah. I'm awake and alert enough to see her." I try to sit up. "Just give me a second....."

"Stay where you are." He puts his hand on my shoulder and pushes me down. "Don't get up."

"Are you sure that's allowed?" I ask. "She's royalty."

He laughs at me. "You better stay down. The family would have a fit if they knew you stood up for one of their visits. I'll go get her."

He walks out and leaves me alone. I want to at least sit up, but I can't even get off the mattress. Forget about getting out of bed.

She enters the room alone. She's wearing one of her usual very nice casual outfits like the one she wore to the mall. She always looks classy and put-together, especially when she leaves the palace.

Her eyes overflow with emotion when she sees me lying down. I see so much in that look. She has feelings for me. No one has to explain this to me. She lets it all pour out of her eyes when she looks at me.

I guess I have feelings for her, too, now that I admit it to myself. I want to tear someone in half for even thinking about her.

"How are you?" she croaks.

"I'm okay," I murmur. "I was so worried about you. Did he....did that guy....did he get inside your apartment?"

"No, not at all!" She gulps to get her voice working. "He ran off after he shot you. I heard the shot and came out and found you. I saw him climbing over the wall and running away. He's locked up now."

I wilt back on my pillow, but she's so beautiful that I can't close my eyes. "Thank goodness. I was worried sick."

She takes a step closer. "Alexei....." She looks down and slips her hand into mine.

I have to squeeze her hand. I don't have the heart to pull away even though I know I should.

Her hand feels small and soft and warm. Everything about her is so unbelievably inviting when she looks at me like this.

She acted so harsh and hateful that first day. I never thought she could be this soft and caring. Now we're bound together by blood and danger. Nothing can break that bond—but everything can break it.

I look up at her and feel my heart break at the look in her eyes. "Listen to me, beautiful angel," I half-whisper. "Nothing can ever happen between us. Do you understand that? You're a princess. I'm a bodyguard. I work for your family. It's impossible. You know that, don't you?"

She looks down at our hands. She doesn't let go. "I don't want to lose you," she husks. "I *can't* lose you—not after all this."

"You might lose me or I might lose you." I have to shut my eyes. "You don't know how much I dread the same thing happening again. It could be you next time. It's my worst nightmare. It would be so much worse if there was anything between us. Imagine how much worse it would be."

Her gaze floats up to mine. Her eyes glisten with emotion, but they don't fill up with tears—not this time. "Is that the only reason?"

I collapse back on the pillow. I'm more exhausted than I realized. "Yes," I whisper. "That's the only reason. I have to keep it professional. I'm here to protect you. I can't take it any further even if I want to."

She stands there in silence for a long time. She doesn't let go of my hand and I don't let go, either. Holding her hand feels too good.

I don't take my eyes off her face. I need to feel this overpowering flood of emotion flowing between us—just once.

She's too important for me to take it any further than this one moment. We'll both go back to our professional relationship and never act on this, but I sense that her feelings won't change even if she backs off.

My feelings won't change, either. She's special to me like no one else I've ever met.

She finally picks up my hand and presses my knuckles to her lips for a long moment before she puts my hand down. "You are a prince, Alexei," she tells me and walks out of the room.

Chapter 14: Simone

I walk into the palace dining room and sit down at the table with my family. Christophe, Pascal, Renáld, and my three cousins talk about the security situation as usual.

"Oh, by the way, Alexei came home today," Christophe announces. "He's staying in his room, but he won't be coming back to work for another week. He still has to recover from his head injury."

"Thank Heaven he's all right," my mother exclaims. "We should do something for him to recognize his heroism."

"I agree with you, but I'm certain he doesn't want that," Christophe replies.

"Of course he doesn't," Salvatore interjects. "He's such a prince."

"I talked to him this morning," Christophe goes on. "He just wants to return to work. He's more concerned about us."

"I hope you didn't tell him about the state dinner on Saturday," my father counters. "It's in three days."

"Unfortunately, he was the one who mentioned it to me. He heard about it at the hospital. He wants to come back to work before then so he can make sure everything is as secure as it can possibly be."

"The dinner won't be as big a problem as it might be," Pascal points out. "It's happening here so we can control the security. It would be worse if we held it anywhere else."

"We'll all be on alert and we're bringing in extra security personnel to patrol the palace that day and all evening," Christophe replies. "I'm sure no one will be surprised to hear that our efforts don't satisfy Alexei. He wants to get involved."

"Why shouldn't he if he's feeling up to it?" my mother asks. "He's supposed to stay off his feet for a week, but he may be feeling stronger by Saturday. Why shouldn't he participate?"

"I should also warn you that he looks different," Christophe adds. "His scar makes him look different."

"Good," Casim interjects. "He was way too good-looking before. He was making the rest of us look bad."

The others laugh. "I'm sorry to disappoint you, but he's still just as good-looking," Christophe replies. "He just looks kind of more dangerous with that scar on his face. He looks like a fighter."

"He is a fighter." The words fall out of my mouth without me meaning to let them. "He was a fighter before—a ferocious fighter."

"Of course he was," Christophe replies. "You'll all see when he comes back to work. I just want to warn you."

"He's more than welcome no matter what he looks like," my mother remarks. "I'm sure his heart is as good as ever."

"I'm sure it is," Christophe replies. "He wouldn't stop talking about all the security measures related to all of us. He's more obsessed with it now than before."

"It's incredible that he's so dedicated to his job," Geneviève interjects. "I never would have believed you could find someone as experienced and dedicated as this."

"I don't think it has anything to do with the job," Christophe replies. "I mean, I'm sure it had everything to do with the job when he came to work here because he's been doing this for decades. Things changed when he came to work for us, though. I don't think it's about the job anymore. I think it's us. He's dedicated to us now. We're what's important to him—making sure we're all safe."

His eyes dart toward me, but only for a split second before he looks away. The conversation shifts to other matters. No one mentions Alexei anymore, but I can't get him out of my mind.

He's right here in the palace. I want to rush off and see him right now, but I can't do that.

Nothing can happen between us. He said it and I know it's true. He's a member of the staff even if everyone treats him like he's part of the family.

He's too professional ever to cross that line—and I would never ask him to violate his integrity like that. He's too honorable.

I know he feels the same way about me. Now we just have to stay in our lanes and not think about each other that way.

I enjoyed a few blissful moments of holding his hand. That's all of him I'll ever get—and it's enough. Just knowing him is enough. Knowing my family is giving him a place in the world—it's enough.

We all know what he's worth. We might be the only people on the planet who truly understand how pure and upright he is.

He belongs here with us. We all admire him too much to let him go anywhere else.

I go back to my apartment and get a visit from Chevalier about the state dinner. This is the first serious function I've attended since the mall shooting.

I haven't wanted to set foot outside the palace, but I've been communicating with my fans online.

The social media world is going crazy with the assassination attempt at the mall. Some people say I got shot. Others say I got killed. I have to quell the rumors, so I do a few live streams where I talk about what happened.

I mention one brave bodyguard who saved my life by stepping in front of the gun, but I don't mention any names.

"You have a wardrobe fitting with Lucille at three o'clock this afternoon," Chevalier tells me. "You can go over any security issues with your outfit then. You're scheduled for a haircut tomorrow at two-thirty and then a manicure on Friday at ten-thirty in the morning."

I turn around in my chair. "What did you say?"

"I said you have a manicure on Friday at ten-thirty in the morning."

"No, before that. You said I could go over any security issues with my outfit at my wardrobe fitting with Lucille."

"Yes, Alexei will meet you there to check the outfit and decide if and what security measures you can take with the fitting. He said to tell you he doesn't know what you're wearing, so he won't be able to recommend anything until he sees it."

"Alexei.....is coming to my wardrobe fitting?! He isn't supposed to be back at work yet."

Chevalier makes a face. "Did any of us really think he would stay in his room for a whole week? He came back to work earlier this morning. I saw him at the security meeting."

I try not to show any agitation at this. I sure hope Alexei isn't putting himself in any kind of danger from his head injury by coming back to work too soon.

I guess I'm about to find out. I go about my business and finally see him in the flesh when I go to meet my family for dinner that evening.

He stands with the others outside the dining room. He's wearing one of his exquisite suits.

Christophe was right about Alexei's appearance. The scar on his face doesn't make him any less good-looking. He's still drop-dead gorgeous, but the scar does make him look dangerous.

He looks like a pirate or a hitman or maybe a crime boss. No one would ever guess he had such a pure, good heart underneath it all.

He stands there talking to my family like he's one of them. "Did you find out how the intruder got over the wall and onto the grounds?" he asks. "I couldn't figure it out. I was wracking my brain in the hospital."

"That guard Carlos sneaked off into the bushes to smoke from his hash pipe," Renáld replies. "We got rid of him by the end of the day."

"Whoa!" Alexei exclaims. "I thought one of the guards had a stroke or passed out on the job or something. I thought all kinds of things. Here I was lying on the ground worried about the guy."

He barely glances at me when I walk up to the group. My father waves us all into the dining room. "Come inside and have dinner with us, Alexei," my father tells him. "I want to talk to you about the state affair on Saturday."

"Oh, no, Your Highness, I couldn't do that," Alexei exclaims. "I'll let you all alone. I have some work to do anyway. You all enjoy your dinner. I'll catch up with you later in the office."

He walks off heading back to the security office. He's probably the only man alive on the planet outside our family who could turn down a dinner invitation from the Crown Prince of Monaco and get away with it.

My father doesn't treat his refusal as anything to remark on. My father waves us all into the dining room and we go sit down.

"We have screeners going through all the catering people, servers, and decorators who will be coming through the palace leading up to the event," Christophe tells us. "The security team will search the dining room and the rest of the palace before and during the dinner to make sure none of the staff are hiding weapons on the premises."

"How did this happen?" my mother asks. "How did our lives turn into this siege?"

"It does seem like there must be some larger force behind all of this," my father remarks. "It doesn't seem possible that all these little Mickey Mouse fringe groups can have built up all this danger so quickly. We never faced anything like this before."

"No larger force made my father hate you and turn my family against you," Geneviève points out. "That was coming for a long time."

"No, of course you're right, my dear," my father tells her. "I didn't mean them."

"If we're right about Blood Tide, then that isn't any hidden force behind it all, either," Pascal interjects. "They're coming after the parties to the Eurasian summit. This has nothing to do with us or Father or Alexei or anyone else."

"Unless Blood Tide is the hidden force behind it all," Salvatore suggests. "Maybe they're the ones coordinating these attacks as well as the hits on the Eurasian summit."

"I wish I could find out what security measures the other heads of state are taking," my father remarks. "Valiyev is the only one Blood Tide actually succeeded in killing, but maybe the other heads of state are going through the same thing. It might help if we compared not es....but I wouldn't want to offend Alexei by asking."

"I doubt he would be offended," Christophe replies. "I'm sure he would be glad to get involved if he thought Blood Tide was behind these attacks. He's as anxious as we are to stop another attack before it happens."

"No, let him alone," my father replies. "He's gone through enough."

Chapter 15: Simone

I walk into the wardrobe fitting room and stop dead in my tracks when I see Alexei in there. He's already wearing the beautiful black tux and bowtie he'll wear to the state dinner tonight. He looks like a much beefier version of James Bond.

He's standing at the clothes rail, taking down dresses, jackets, skirts, and tops, inspecting each one, and putting them back before he takes another.

His eyes soften when he looks up and sees me. "Hi," I murmur.

"Hello. I'm here to do my security assessment on your outfit for the dinner. Do you know what you're wearing?"

I nod and cross to the rail. I have to stand next to him to take down the dress I'll be wearing.

Standing this close to him makes my heart flutter, but I can't do anything with him—now or ever.

Lucille seals the deal by walking in from the other room just then. She glares at Alexei, but she doesn't comment on him being here.

The whole staff knows about him now. The family and staff know enough to respect him. My father and brothers can't stop talking about him.

Lucille barges over to us and takes down my dress before I can show it to Alexei.

"You should try it on first so we know if I need to take it in." She holds the dress up in front of me. It's a sheer, copper gown with sleek, hugging curves and a scoop neckline that shows off my chest. "Then I can alter it while you get your hair and makeup done."

She holds the dress out to me, but Alexei takes it out of her hands first. She glares at him again when he rubs the fabric between his fingers, turns the dress around from back to front, and even spreads open the neckline so he can look down inside it.

"It doesn't look like we'll be able to reinforce this the way we did with your jacket," he tells me.

"What do you want to do about that?" I ask.

"We might not be able to do anything about it. What shapewear are you wearing underneath the dress?"

I take him to the other side of the room and show him the waist trainer and shaping body stocking I'll be wearing under the dress. They won't show.

He feels the fabric on those, too. "No, we won't be able to reinforce these, either. They won't cover your vital organs anyway, so you'll just have to wear them the way they are."

"How will you mitigate the risks?" I ask.

"I'll escort you. I'll be staying extra close to you for the evening, so be prepared for that."

"Good. I'm relieved." I take the shapewear out of his hands. "I better go put these on. Are you sticking around for me to get my hair and makeup done?"

He nods. "The hair and makeup people are new. We screened them, but we still have to be careful in case someone slips through."

"I'll just try on my dress for Lucille and then we can go next door."

I take the dress and the shapewear into the dressing room, put everything on, and step outside. Lucille moves in and starts adjusting the dress.

I squirm in the slippery fabric. I become aware of Alexei watching me. His eyes trace down my body, over my hips, thighs, arms, and bust. He sees everything. This dress hides nothing.

I can't trick myself into believing he's only looking to assess how safe I'll be. He's checking me out.

He confirms it when his eyes snap up to meet mine before he looks away. He doesn't look at me again while Lucille pins up my dress. Then I have to take it off.

Alexei only lets himself look at me once I change back into my regular clothes. We go next door.

I sit in the chair in front of the dressing table while the hair stylist and makeup artist get me ready for the state dinner tonight. Alexei does a much more thorough job of checking out all their stuff while they work.

He makes them both nervous by rummaging in the hair stylist's tool trays and searching the makeup artist's box of makeup. Alexei opens multiple tubes of mascara, eyeshadow, and concealer, smells them, and reads the labels.

The makeup artist casts terrified glances at him over her shoulder when he even dabs some of the mascara on a tissue to check its consistency.

He makes half a dozen circuits of the room looking into corners and glaring out the windows.

His behavior makes me feel better. I don't want him anywhere else but right next to me tonight—and not because I'm starting to have feelings for him—or not only because of that.

Thank the stars in heaven he'll be there. He'll handle anything that happens. He's taking every possible step to make sure nothing happens.

Security has been off the charts the last three days leading up to this event. Alexei has been working tirelessly with my brothers and the rest of the security team.

Christophe wasn't fooling around when he said they would search every room in the palace again and again for any sign of danger. The attackers hiding the weapon under the dinner table last time puts everyone on edge.

I sit in silence and stare straight in front of me. I don't comment on Alexei's attention to every detail of what the hair stylist and makeup artist are doing.

The hair stylist messes up one time, accidentally drops the brush, and it gets tangled in my hair. I wince when it snarls.

She apologizes and starts detangling it, but not before Alexei comes over. He hovers over her and me for the whole process.

She's a nervous wreck by the time she straightens out my hair and goes back to brushing it. I don't blame her for being nervous, but I can't bring myself to resent anything he does. Any of these people could be trying to infiltrate the palace to attack us.

I wait for them to finish and go back to the fitting room to get dressed for the evening. Alexei checks out my dress again, but he does it more professionally this time. No one would ever know something passed between us.

Maybe nothing passed between us, but things can't go back to the way they were—not for me, at least. I don't know exactly how he feels about me, but I know how I feel about him.

I finally slip my feet into my shoes. I stand a few inches taller once I put them on.

Alexei comes over to me and lowers his voice to an intimate murmur. "Stay close to me tonight, okay? Don't wander off."

"I won't. I don't want to."

"Come on. Let's go." He picks up my hand and places it through his arm so it looks like he's escorting me. He is escorting me.

He doesn't look like a bodyguard. He looks like my date—or I should say he wouldn't look like a bodyguard if not for that scar on his face.

It makes him look much more distinguished somehow. It's a mark of his experience and resilience. He's tough. That's what Christophe says and it's true.

We head down the halls, but we don't go into the dining room. I hear people in there talking and laughing.

The waiters come and go from the kitchens. Security guards flow into and out of the dining room—and every other room in the palace.

Alexei and I enter one of the nearby parlors. My family is in there waiting for us. Geneviève and Emeline sit on a couch with my mother. Everyone else stands.

My father kisses me on the cheek. "You look magnificent, my dear—and so do you, my boy." My father pats Alexei on the shoulder.

"Thank you, Your Highness," Alexei replies. "I better look good if I'm escorting this radiant creature."

"Creature!" I gasp. "I'm scandalized."

Alexei laughs and so does my father. "We can change it to 'bird' if you want to. Isn't that what the English say? They call a young lady a bird."

"That's different," I tell him. "That's an insult."

"No, it isn't," Alexei chimes in. "It's just another word for a young woman—like 'sheila' is to the Australians or 'chick' is to the Americans."

That makes both me and my father laugh. "There must be some relation between the English birds and the American chicks—maybe because one is older than the other."

Alexei grins at me and his cheeks blush. "I wouldn't know anything about that. Words aren't my specialty."

I smile back at him, but it's just a friendly smile. This is the friendliest we've ever acted toward each other.

We have to pay attention when Chevalier comes to tell us it's time for us to enter the dining room. The security team has held back the Royal Family until now.

More security guards are escorting Emeline, Daphne, Johanne, and Marguerite. Each of my brothers and male cousins has a guard assigned to them, too, but none of the guards hover as closely.

Emeline, Marguerite, and my two female cousins all wear much thicker gowns that cover more of their bodies. I can't be sure, but I bet each of them is wearing some reinforcement under or inside their clothes.

All the men wear bulletproof vests under their tuxes. So does Alexei and so does my father.

Christophe and Geneviève go first. The rest of us follow in no particular order. I slip my hand back into Alexei's elbow. Standing this close to him feels like the safest place in the world.

He matches his step to mine even though he's so much taller. We head down the hall and enter the dining room. All the other guests are already in there.

Chapter 16: Simone

M y family and I spread out through the dining room to greet as many guests as possible. The security guards keep an ever-present watch on all of us every minute.

More of them come into and out of the dining room, check everything out, and use the crowd to cover up the fact that they're searching the room even now.

One of the guards checks out the silverware on the table and "accidentally" drops one of the spoons on the floor. He bends down to pick it up and happens to glance upward while he's down there to check the underside of the table.

Other guards migrate through the room greeting everyone and commenting on their stunning outfits. The guards take advantage of the conversations to look more closely at everyone without actually searching them for concealed weapons.

My mother is right. The whole palace is turning into a fortress, but those of us in the Royal Family are the only ones who realize it. None of these people see anything other than a bunch of men in tuxes who might be any other guests.

Christophe and the team have even hired a bunch of female security professionals just for tonight to pose as our regular guards' dates. The women all wear immaculate evening gowns, but each one has their outfit tailored to conceal at least one weapon.

I don't let go of Alexei's elbow even once. I stop in front of Anaïs RobillardShe's Serge Robillard's wife. He's the ambassador to Luxembourg.

She clasps my hand and kisses me on the cheek. "It's wonderful to see you so well after all that drama." She laughs and turns to Alexei. "And who is this magnificent specimen? I didn't hear that you were dating anyone, my dear."

"This isn't my date. This is Alexei Asatiani. He's our new chief of security. He's acting as my bodyguard for tonight."

She pats my arm. "He should have been your date." She holds out her hand to him. "Welcome, my dear. You look smashing."

"Thank you, Madame," he replies. "So do you."

She laughs and blushes at him. "I'm sure you say that to all the ladies."

"It's part of my job, Madame," he tells her and makes her laugh again.

We work our way through the room socializing and exchanging political gossip here and there. Anaïs Robillard isn't the only one who mistakes Alexei for my date. If only he was.

He never leaves my side even, but I still see him casting hard glances around. I look up at him once. "Is everything all right?"

He gives me one short nod. "So far. Let's keep it that way."

We don't talk again until a commotion breaks out behind us. A flurry of excitement goes through the hall when my parents walk in. Their own cluster of four security guards surround them on all sides.

The guests make a fuss over my parents. Some try to get near them to greet them, but the security guards stop anyone from getting too close.

My father smiles, nods, and greets everyone, but he doesn't stop walking. He escorts my mother to the head of the table.

That's the signal for everyone to sit down. Alexei ushers me to my seat and pulls my chair out for me, but he doesn't sit down. He isn't here as a guest.

He plants himself behind my chair, folds his hands in front of him, and casts his sharp eyes up and down the table for any sign of danger.

The other guests move in and everyone starts sitting down. The servers, waiters, and butlers also enter and stand in readiness at the other end of the hall.

The servers and waiters hold silver-covered trays to serve us as soon as everyone settles down.

I'm one of the first to take my seat. The others shuffle themselves around. The security guards advance toward the table, and right then, one of the servers drops his tray.

It hits the floor with a deafening crash, but he's already pulling two machine guns from under his jacket. Three other servers do exactly the same thing.

Alexei dives for me just as the gunmen open fire down the table. Their position gives them a clear shot straight down the table to the Crown Prince and Princess sitting at the far end.

Alexei collides with me and smashes my chair over even before the gunfire can erupt. We crashed down hard on the floor as bullets rupture the table, the china, all the fancy glasswork, the flower arrangements, and the bullets hit bodies right and left.

I scream, but it's all on now. Alexei seizes me in his arms, hurls himself sideways, and rolls under the table as machine gunfire destroys the dining room.

Security guards in tuxes stalk past us to corner the gunmen. I don't see anything else.

Screams, shattering glass, and splintering wood mix into a confused torrent of ear-splitting noise. I cower on the floor, clamp my hands over my ears, and huddle for cover.

Alexei lies on top of me crushing me in his arms. The only place to hide is under his big, muscular frame.

I put my head down and wind up resting it against his chest. He doesn't push me away. He closes his hand on the back of my head and pulls me in tighter.

Bullets whistle and zing all over the room. I don't dare to look out in case one of those projectiles hits me.

I'm still screaming in terror when Alexei pries himself off me. "Come on!" he yells at me. "We gotta get out of here!"

"How?!" I yell back. "We can't!!"

"Come with me—now, Simone!"

My past experience taught me to always follow his instructions. He rolls off me, pushes himself back onto his heels under the table, and draws both sidearms from under his jacket.

He glances around. I can't tell where all the shooting is coming from.

Actually, now that I think about it, all the shooting seems to be coming from the dining room entrance doors.

Alexei yells one more time, "Stay with me! Don't fall behind!"

He pulls me up, pushes me onto all fours, and steers me toward the far end of the table.

I don't see my parents down there. I don't know who is even still in this dining hall, but Alexei and I are the only ones under the table or down on the floor. I sure hope my family is all right.

A few dead bodies slump in their chairs where they were just sitting down or they sprawl on the floor with blood pooling around them. I don't dare to check if any of those people are members of my family.

Alexei doesn't let me check or even look around. We both crawl under the table getting farther away from the gun battle raging near the doors.

I stop at the end of the table and we both look behind us. I can't tell which side is which or who's doing what.

Alexei doesn't put his guns down. He crawls out from under the table, peeks above it, and waves his gun for me to move forward.

I crawl out there, but only because he's there. I wouldn't if he wasn't here. He turns around. "Get ready to run when I say, okay?" he yells in my ear.

I nod even though I'm not ready to run.

"NOW!!" he roars.

He doesn't wait for me to get to my feet. He grabs me by the arms from behind, lifts me up, and holds me tight against his body in a low, stooping crouch.

We dart across the room and plunge through a side door leading to the butler's pantry and the kitchens. He shoves me through the door and doesn't slow down before he turns a corner.

The kitchens have been swarming with security guards in the lead-up to this dinner. We turn the corner and see a bunch of men in tuxes, but they aren't our security guys.

These are servers, waiters, and other members of the catering team. My brothers have spent two weeks screening and vetting all these people.

Alexei and I ought to be safe here, but all those guys carry machine guns. The intruders don't even carry their weapons under their clothes now.

They spot us and yells echo through the kitchen when all the invaders come after us. Some of the gunmen draw their weapons to mow us down right here and now.

Alexei pushes me down a different hall and unloads his sidearms at the gunmen before charging after me. We race away and turn a bunch of corners before we skid into the main palace corridor.

We blunder into another major gun battle between our security team on one side and the armed intruders on the other. It's hard to tell one side from the other when everyone is wearing a tux.

A few women in evening gowns fight on one side. That's the only difference.

Bullets rip and ricochet up the corridor and almost cut me and Alexei in half. He dives back to block me from going out there, but more gunmen come up behind us. They know where we are now.

Alexei grabs me, spins me away, and we take off in another direction toward my father's reception hall. He usually conducts official state business there.

Shouting voices follow us. Will we ever find safety? Is anywhere in the world safe anymore?

We can only keep running, but Alexei pulls me sideways after just a few minutes. He yanks open a broom closet, shoves me inside, and crowds in with me before he shuts the door.

Darkness falls over both of us. A crack of light angles through the gap under the door. It casts the broom closet in an eerie glow.

I get a flashback of his phone at the country house. He's taking care of me again. He doesn't care about anything except that we both get out of here alive.

Chapter 17: Alexei

Simone and I gasp and pant for air. We're both sweating and breathing heavily after escaping from the dining room, but we aren't free yet. Armed gunmen are invading the palace.

They shot up the dining room. Now they're out there fighting the palace security team.

I should go out there and help them, but Simone is my top priority.

I would have to leave her unattended if I went out there. Then something might happen to me and she would be utterly alone. I can't let that happen.

I have to smash my body right up against her so we both fit inside the broom closet. I shouldn't be touching her like this and even pressing my body against her, but I don't have a choice.

I look down into her eyes. Her angelic face hovers right in front of me close enough to kiss. We might as well be making out in this closet, but we have to catch and hold our breath when we hear people rushing back and forth right outside the door.

Feet and legs break the light sneaking through the gap under the door. Simone and I stare at each other when we hear the gunmen yelling. They're looking for us. They know we came this way.

Neither of us says a word or makes a sound. I don't dare to breathe, but I have to. I breathe through my nose so they don't hear me.

I realize I'm still crushing both my sidearms in my hands. I don't want to put them away in case I need them.

Simone must have torn her dress when she crawled under the table. Dust and plaster chalk cover most of it and the silky fabric has ripped up her side to reveal her bra. I pretend not to notice.

I also pretend not to notice her cleavage pressing right against my jacket. I can look straight down between her breasts from this position.

I shouldn't think of her that way, but my mind starts playing tricks on me. I feel my body starting to respond. I look away, but it doesn't help.

Her presence electrifies me. I need to get out of this closet before I do something I might regret.

I can't do anything with her. She's a princess of Monaco. I can never be anything to her but her bodyguard. She might have a fling with me, but that's it.

I could ruin my reputation and my career if I crossed that line. Besides, I respect her too much. She deserves someone so much better—someone richer and more influential that she can build a future with. That is never going to be me.

Just keeping her alive in the palace right now is going to be challenging enough. The gunmen run back and forth out there and then all sound fades from the hallway.

I have to take a chance at getting Simone out of here before the gunmen come back. I still hear gunfire belching out of sight.

I raise my finger to my lips to keep her quiet. She nods.

I ease the door open, take a look outside, and then grab her hand to pull her into the open. We take off running the way we were going before.

We're heading for the Royal Family's apartments, but we almost get discovered when the gunmen come out of there. They must be searching all the apartments trying to find everyone.

I dive into a different apartment just as the gunmen approach it to search it. I tackle Simone again, but I don't slam her down as hard as last time.

We roll under the bed just in time. The gunmen storm in behind us and start searching the place. The sheets, bedspread, and valance on the bed hide us under here for now.

I pivot onto my other side and hold the gunmen's footsteps at gunpoint while they search the apartment. They'll get a face full of lead if even one of them looks under the bed.

I'm lying here holding my breath in tense anticipation when Simone scoots in behind me, slips her arms around my waist from behind, and presses her face against my back.

She flattens her hands against my chest. Her touch sends a bolt of lightning through me. She isn't holding onto me because we're trapped here and hiding from armed gunmen.

Her arms feel blissfully soft and comforting. They relax me instantly, but her touch also erupts protective feelings for her. No one is going to harm her as long as I'm around.

I don't turn over. I shouldn't let myself feel this, but it's already too late.

She lifts her face and kisses the back of my neck. That kiss speaks volumes. She *is* holding me like this because we're trapped and hiding from armed gunmen.

This might be our only chance. It *will* be our only chance. We might end up dead in a few minutes—or we might make it out of here and find our way back to her family.

We'll never be together—not really. We'll never get a chance to explore what might happen between us if we were anyone else in the world.

The gunmen leave, but I don't get out from under the bed. I stay where I am and sink into the feeling of her holding me.

Her pure care and affection floods me from her arms. She admires me. She likes me for who I am. That's all this is. She just wants to express how she feels. I can't break that.

I feel the same way about her. She's beautiful all the way down to her soul, but she can never be mine.

I finally let myself turn over and face her. Every brain cell I possess tells me to end this now before it goes any further. Everything else that I am tells me to take this chance because it will never come again.

She loosens her arms when I turn over. She doesn't try to hold onto me. She already knows nothing can happen between us. She held me for one minute. She doesn't think it can ever be more than that.

I can't hold back from doing the same thing when I see her eyes glistening up at me. She doesn't cry or wince or anything like that. She just looks at me.

She looks at me like she doesn't want to stop looking at me. She looks at me as if someone is going to come along any second now and tell her to stop looking at me.

She looks at me in the way she can't look at me when everyone else is around to see her looking at me that way.

I put one of my sidearms down on the floor so I can lay my hand against her cheek. I need to show her how I feel, too, even if it only lasts a few seconds. I'll never get another chance.

I lean in and kiss her. I don't need anything else but this moment right here.

Her lips melt against mine. They feel velvet-soft and angelically magical—just like the rest of her.

I just plan to give her one kiss, but as soon as I do, her hands fly to my waist. She doesn't touch me in any other way, but that one touch breaks something in me.

I kiss her deeper and she responds. I can't stop it. I kiss her faster and harder. Our tongues meet and I grab her in my arms to pull her close.

We both fall deep, deep into kissing each other as if this will never end. It will end. It will end sooner than either of us want.

I can't stop. I won't stop. I don't want to stop not even when the gunmen find us and kill us both. I hope I die kissing her.

Her luscious body falls effortlessly into my arms. She undulates that long satin dress down my suit exactly the way I imagined in the wardrobe fitting room.

Her body charges with electric energy when I glide my hands down her sides. Her breath quickens in my nostrils and she presses herself tighter against me.

That feeling that I want her turns me on. I feel myself getting hard for her and I try to hold back, but she feels it, too, and rubs herself against me even more to drive me wild.

I have to resist the urge to grab her ass and crush her against my crotch. I want to more than anything, but I can't treat her like that. She's a princess. I couldn't do that to her no matter how hot she is.

I can't grab her breasts and rip her top down, either. Thinking that blasts my mind apart. I'm going crazy here.

She slides her hands up my back and trails her fingers through my hair and down my neck. I want to tear her apart, but I control myself enough not to.

I satisfy myself with sliding my hand up her back, cradling her neck, and tangling my fingers in her hair. She's already messy enough. I don't have to worry about anyone seeing her all done up.

She mews into my mouth when I steer her lips deep into my kiss—as deep as I can get her. I want to take her right now—but I want more than that.

It twists the knife in my guts that I can never have her. I can never be the man she needs me to be. I'm not here for that.

I'm here to protect her—that's all. Someone else will be the man in her life and I'll become nothing, which is what I am.

Her passion blows my mind. She never stops kissing me or pulls away or even eases off—unless I do it first. She kisses me fully, deliciously, and with all her heart and soul.

She holds nothing back from that kiss and her eyes float open with so much desire and emotion pouring out of her. She wants me in the same way. I see that written in her eyes. She wants me to be the man in her life, but that can never happen.

We lie there in silence staring into each other's eyes. I want to say so much to her, but I don't dare to say a word.

She strokes my cheeks, rubs the back of my neck, and presses her delicate hand against my chest. I'm wearing a bulletproof vest, but that touch means so much.

She would touch and kiss me like this if we could ever find a way to be together. She would look at me like this—like she can't live without me.

How can I ever let this woman go? How can I stand by and watch her spend her life with another man?

That's exactly what I will do because she deserves the best. She deserves the best man in her life and she deserves the best bodyguard. That's what I am and that's all I have to give her.

I kiss her one last time before I leave here to get her to safety. I don't know where that is, but I'll have to find something.

Our lips join while we're still gazing into each other's eyes. I never want to look away.

My body takes over and I roll on top of her. I want to feel this—just once. I want to feel what it would be like if she was really mine.

She whimpers softly enough that no one can hear her. Her eyes fly open with such a look of agonized longing. I would give anything to take her right now, but I have to stop this before it goes too far.

I feel her trembling with overflowing, insatiable desire—and then I roll off her. I can't keep torturing myself like this.

I give her one more kiss and pull her toward the edge of the bed so we can get out of here—and right then my phone buzzes in my pocket.

Chapter 18: Alexei

I pull my phone out of my pocket and check the screen. I put the phone on vibrate for the state dinner. It doesn't make any noise.

Christophe is calling me, but I don't dare to answer. I wouldn't be able to talk to him—not without attracting the intruders' attention.

I decline the call and then text him. *Simone and I are hiding. I can't talk to you right now.*

He writes back immediately. *Where are you?*

We're hiding under the bed in one of the guest apartments. Where are you?

The security team got us out and took us to a secure location.

Give me directions so I can take Simone there. The gunmen are still all over the place. I don't want them to find us.

The gunbattle is still going on—or it's going off and on. Our people are still trying to drive everyone out of the palace. It won't be safe for you to come here. I want you to take Simone somewhere else. Take her out of the palace.

How can I? I ask. *The gunmen would see us.*

Go to the far end of the corridor. You'll find a cleaner's closet next to the front door of my parents' apartment. You'll find a ring set into the floor of the closet. Lift out the floor panel and go down the stairs into the hidden tunnels under the palace. They'll lead you to a safe house in the city. I want you to take Simone there and DO NOT bring her back to the palace, Alexei. Do you understand? Don't bring her back under any circumstances until you hear from me that it's safe.

I understand. I just feel bad for running away and leaving all of you here to deal with the intruders.

Simone's safety is more important. Do as I say, Alexei. Take Simone to safety and don't you dare leave her alone even for a second. I'm trusting you with her safety.

I understand. Just tell me you and all the rest of your family are okay.

We're fine for now. We were worried about you and Simone. We had no idea if you even made it out of the dining room alive.

We're both fine. Neither of us is hurt. We just have to stay hidden so the gunmen don't find us.

Wait until they leave and then get down the hall to the cleaner's closet. You should be fine after that.

Okay, I tell him. *I'll try to contact you once we get to the safe house.*

Okay. Good luck. Our thoughts go with you.

I put my phone away and look up to find Simone watching me. Does she know about the tunnels and the safe house? She's about to find out.

I scoot out from under the bed and hold my breath to listen. I don't hear anyone moving around nearby.

I wave her out and holster one of my guns so I can take her hand. I can't let her get too far away from me. I need to keep her with me at all costs in case I need to stop someone from shooting her again.

We tiptoe to the door. I don't hear anyone out there, either. I ease the door open. The corridor is empty.

I pull the door open, step out into the corridor, and start to back away toward the Crown Prince's apartment.

He and Princess Jasmine live in a massive apartment at the far end of this wing. Their children each have their own apartments in the same wing in descending order of age.

I pass my weapon back and forth in every direction, but I don't see or hear a thing. My heart pounds nearly out of my chest as I count down the seconds until we get away.

I start to turn around when I hear voices. They're coming toward this wing from another part of the palace. I push Simone away just as another squad of armed intruders stroll around that corner on their way somewhere else.

They aren't looking for us. They aren't looking for anything. One of them looks over his shoulder while he talks to his friends.

The others spot us, yell out, and grab for their weapons. I push Simone toward the cleaner's closet, but I realize in that moment that I can't take her there—not now.

The intruders would see us. Then they would know where we were. They would follow us and probably gun us down.

Simone stumbles away. She ditched her high heels somewhere along the way. I can't remember where, but she can move a lot better like this.

She doesn't head for the cleaner's closet. She doesn't know we're supposed to go there.

I spin around and both the intruders and I open fire at the same instant. They spray bullets all over the corridor and nearly cut down me and Simone.

She trips, falls, and I have to leap over her so I don't step on her. I snatch her by the hand and slide her across the floor toward the nearest open door. It leads into Christophe's and Geneviève's apartment.

I barely bundle Simone inside and lean out just long enough to shoot back and hold the intruders at bay. They're making their way up the corridor heading straight for us. They know exactly where we are.

I grab Simone and pull her to her feet. I was trying to get to the Crown Prince's apartment, but this one will have to be good enough. It *is* good enough for what I want.

I shove Simone away from the door. "Get out into the grounds! Go!"

She charges away from me and gets to the patio doors first. I dive for cover when the gunmen open fire on me again.

I slam the door shut and haul the side table in front of it. That won't hold them off for long. I have to act fast.

Simone pulls the doors open and waits for me to catch up with her. We both dive out into the grounds and cross the patio just as the gunmen force their way into the apartment behind us.

They yell to each other and more gunmen gather from all over. Simone is the only member of the Royal Family left in the palace. The gunmen will hunt us down until they finish us off.

More gunmen rush in from all over the grounds. Jesus, they're everywhere!

I dive behind one of the hedges and push her along to the end where it meets up with the rose garden. We both sprint through it to another hedge maze. We should be able to lose the intruders here.

She's panting hard, but she doesn't slow down for a second. We skim through the maze. I make a few wrong turns and she pulls me in different directions until we come out in a different part of the grounds.

She wants to run away, but I pull her back toward her parents' apartment. She shakes her head. I nod, grab her hand, and make her come with me. She cooperates, thank God.

I have to slow myself down so I can open the Crown Prince's patio doors without making any sound. I shut them behind Simone so the intruders don't realize where we went.

We slip through the giant bedroom, cross the palatial living room, and I peek through the door back into the hall. The coast is clear to the cleaner's closet. I pull the door the rest of the way open.

Simone does everything I ask when I draw her into the corridor, pull open the closet door, and push her inside.

We have to cram against each other again when I shut the door behind me. She spreads her hands in a silent gesture to ask why we're in here when we had a clear run to get away across the grounds.

I lift her up and sit her on the cleaner's workbench. I have to move a few things around and be sure to do it silently so I can raise the floor panel leading to the stairs.

I guide her down first and then slowly, gently, silently lower the panel on top of us.

No light makes it down here into the tunnel. It smells of damp stone and mildew.

"Where are you?" Simone whispers.

I wave my hands around until I touch her. I take her hand. "Hold onto me," I whisper back. "I'll guide us along the wall. Come on."

I holster my guns, take her hand, and use my other hand to follow the wall. I have no idea where I'm going, but at least we're out of the palace. We put more and more distance between us and the gunmen every minute we stay free.

I make sure to walk this time. Both Simone and I need to catch our breath.

She sticks close to my side all the way. "How did you find out about this place?" she whispers.

"That was Christophe on the phone earlier. He told me to get you out of the palace. This tunnel leads to a safe house." I glance behind me. "At least I hope it does."

Chapter 19: Simone

A lexei and I don't talk on our way down the long, dark, damp tunnel leading away from the palace. We got away from the gunmen. Now we just have to find a safe place to hide out and regroup.

I don't even want to know what Christophe told Alexei on the phone about what happened to my family. Am I the last member of the Royal Family still alive?

I can't be because Christophe called Alexei to tell him about this tunnel. Someone is still alive somewhere. I'm not completely alone.

Thank all the stars in heaven that Alexei is here. I never want to let go of his hand.

We spot a glimmer of light ahead and Alexei heads for it. We wind up standing under a drain grate in a street somewhere out in the city.

We both look up at daylight outside. We can hear cars driving down the street, people walking past, and others talking in the distance.

Neither of us moves for a second. I don't want to believe this is real. We're outside. We're out in the real world with real people.

None of these people knows what's going on inside the palace just a few blocks away.

I'm still looking up at the sky overhead when Alexei lowers his eyes and looks at me. His eyes dip to my dress, but not the way they did before.

"We need to get you some different clothes," he murmurs. "We need to disguise you so people don't recognize you."

"How do we do that without going out onto the street?"

"I'm not sure, but we can't let anyone find out that you made it out of the palace or where you're going. That's exactly what we don't want." He looks down at his suit. "I guess we need to get me some different clothes, too."

He starts attacking his immaculate tux. It isn't so immaculate anymore. Dust and muck covers him all over.

He tears off his bowtie and throws it on the ground followed by his jacket. He takes off his shoulder holster harness and pulls off his shirt. He's wearing another grey T-shirt underneath with his bulletproof vest over it.

"Stay here," he tells me while he takes his clothes off. "Do NOT show your face up there dressed like that. Understand? The intruders could have stationed people all over the neighborhood. Stay down here and make sure you're here when I come back."

"Of course," I tell him. "I'll be here."

He rips the Velcro straps off his vest to take that off, too, looks around again, and then rubs his hands all over the stone tunnel walls. He covers them in dirt, smudges up his face and arms, and even runs some of the muck through his hair.

He smirks at me when he finishes. "What do you think? Do I look like a palace bodyguard now?"

I stifle a laugh. "No, not at all. You look like a homeless guy—except that you're way too muscular."

He kicks off his shoes and peels off his socks. "How about now?"

I nod and wind up blushing at him. "Better."

"Hopefully no one looks too closely. Stay here, okay?"

"I will."

He raises his burly arms. He looks so different like this. I would never pick him out as a palace bodyguard.

I retreat into the shadows when he lifts out the grate above our heads. His warning sinks home. I don't want anyone seeing me dressed like this. I don't want anyone seeing me at all.

He tells me, "I'll be right back," pulls himself out onto the street, and lowers the grate back into place to conceal me.

I sink back against the wall after he vanishes out of sight. I don't know what he'll do out there or when he'll come back, but I trust him with my life. I would be stupid not to.

I have to stop myself from pacing around. I should sit down.

This dress is the worst outfit to get stranded in—either somewhere I don't want to be seen or somewhere I don't care if I'm seen. It's the most impractical outfit I've ever worn.

At least I'm not wearing my heels anymore. I left them behind in the dining room. I never could have run all over the palace and the grounds in those.

Alexei comes back a few minutes later, lifts out the grate, climbs down holding a bundle under his arms, and puts the grate back.

"Here. You can change into these." He unwraps the bundle and reveals a pair of enormous baggy pants, a giant green hoodie with, *NOTRE DAME,* emblazoned across the front, a wooly ski hat, and a pair of black and white sneakers.

I laugh when I see the clothes. "This is definitely not my recognizable style."

"That's the point. I'll turn around while you change."

He starts to turn his back on me. I stop him by laying my hand on his arm.

We just made out under the bed. I would have gone a lot farther with him, but I understand why he doesn't want to.

We're on the run for our lives. I don't want to keep any secrets from him, especially not how I feel about him.

I turn him around to face me and hold his eyes with mine while I unzip my dress in the back.

It falls away to reveal my bra and all my shapewear underneath. I slide my waist trainer off and then peel off my bodysuit until I'm standing in front of him in my black lacy bra and panties.

I straighten up so he can see all of me at once. I'm about to cover up with all those oversized clothes. I want him to see me now, even if it's the only time.

He lets his gaze migrate all over me. He doesn't stop staring. He feasts his gaze on me taking in every curve and detail. His gaze turns me on.

I want to feel him touching me the way he did under the bed. I want his hands on me and his body on top of me. I want all of that right here in this tunnel.

It will probably never happen. We both know better than to go there, but before I can turn away to put on the hoodie, he leans forward and grabs me.

He scoops his muscular arm behind my back, smashes my lips under his mouth, and attacks me kissing and hauling me toward him in rabid desire.

I fall against him wearing nothing but my bra and panties now. He feels rock solid with only his thin T-shirt between us.

He crushes me down on the rigid spike under his pants. He collapses back against the wall and pulls me down onto his lap.

He doesn't hold anything back this time. He grabs my ass, pulls my thighs around him, and grabs my breasts through my bra.

I squeal into his mouth and then moan as he rocks me against his hard prick. I spiral into a drunken haze of maddening desire and deep need to feel him inside me.

His shoulders swell under his T-shirt. I know what he looks like under there. I want to touch his skin and feel how strong he is, but he mauls me too fast, dives his hot mouth against my neck, and gnaws his way down to my chest.

I yelp out in ecstasy when he nuzzles me through my bra. He keeps kneading my ass and guiding me in scorching rhythm on his hips. I can't hold back. I feel like I'm about to scream.

He tears me off, stands me up, and turns me around to push me against the wall. I don't care if I get dirty as long as I'm with him.

He grabs both my wrists, pins them against the wall, and holds me there while he devours my mouth and crushes me under his weight.

He doesn't pull away from letting me feel every inch of his iron hardness under his clothes—his chest, his hands, his hips, his shaft....

His breath strains with every undulating wave of his muscles. I get lost in the vast bliss of feeling him control me and pin me down. He can be so gentle, but he has another side he never shows anyone.

I would love to let that part of him out of its cage. I would love to feel it unleash on me and take me to the heights of pleasure.

He lets go of one of my wrists and finally pulverizes my breasts in his powerful fingers. He pulls my bra down and digs his fingers inside to torture my nipples. He makes me scream into his mouth. I'm spiraling too fast to stop.

That's the moment when he drives his knee between my legs and rides it hard against my panties. I can't hold back. I scream out in one excruciating climax and buckle in spasms of ragged ecstasy.

He keeps grinding on me as long as the tempest lasts. He reads me exactly and stops as soon as I start to come down.

He circles my waist from behind again, lifts me in his giant arms, and pulls my legs around his waist to hold me against him in the middle of the tunnel.

I crumble on his shoulder whimpering and moaning as the wave rushes through me again and again as it subsides. I cling to him for all I'm worth.

He holds me tight against him and covers my face and hair with kisses while I shudder and sob in his arms. I never want to let go of him even though I know I have to.

He strokes my hair and cradles me in such tenderness compared to how fierce and aggressive he got just a few seconds ago. He lets his own passion die and becomes again the gentle protector I know so well.

I hide in his neck from the emotion breaking me apart. I just want him. I want all of him all to myself. I can't stand the thought that I want him and can't have him.

He's holding me in my bra and panties. He could have taken me right now and I would have loved every second of it.

I want to lose myself in him. I want to get lost in all the mysteries of his body discovering my body. I want to feel his heart pumping into mine.

Holding him like this only confirms that he'll never be mine and I'll never be his. That's the one unbreakable law between us.

This moment—today—all these precious encounters we're sharing—they can only happen because it's today. We're alone and we both might wind up dead tomorrow. That's the only reason either of us can do this now.

He holds me in the silence for a long time. I don't want to leave this little bubble of safety.

Chapter 20: Simone

Alexei eventually sits down on the floor, settles me on his lap with my legs still wrapped around his waist, and pulls my head down on his shoulder. He doesn't make me sit up or function or face the world. I can't do any of those things right now.

I drift off into a dream world. I lose track of time before I come back to my senses enough to lift my head.

Alexei strokes my face to brush my hair back. "How do you feel?" he murmurs.

"Exhausted," I croak. "I can't do any more running or hiding or getting shot at."

He smiles so kindly. "You don't have to. The safe house is right on the corner. No one will recognize you. We can walk there, go upstairs, and no one will ever find us."

I gulp and force myself to look around. "How do you know where it is?"

"Christophe told me. I texted him again when I went outside."

He picks up the bulletproof vest, pulls all the Velcro straps loose, and tightens it around my body over my bra. Then he opens my hoodie, puts his hands inside it, and pulls it over my head.

He won't stop touching me, caressing my hair back into place, and rubbing my arms through the thick fabric.

He kisses me once before he pulls the hat down over my head. He finger-combs my hair into place around my cheeks. I don't even want to know what I look like.

I see reflected in his eyes that he still thinks I'm as beautiful as ever. That's the thing about him. He doesn't care what I look like. He'll always take care of me.

I can't keep sitting here when we're in danger. The allure of finally getting somewhere safe overrides everything else.

We both act at the same time. He lifts me up and I stand on my own feet before I put on the pants and stick my feet into the sneakers.

I have to roll down the waistband of the pants so they don't fall down around my ankles. Then I tie the shoes.

"Should I smudge up my face, too?" I ask.

He laughs. "You don't have to. I think you're unrecognizable enough as you are—but you can if you really want to. I bet you've never been dirty in your life, have you?"

"Are you kidding? Antoinette would have a heart attack if I got a speck of dirt under my nails."

He laughs again. "Too bad. You would look cute all smudged up. In fact....."

He sticks out his finger, collects a blob of muck from the wall, and moves his finger close to my nose. I dodge just in time and push his hand away. "You better knock it off," I tell him. "I know your boss, remember?

He only laughs and uses his finger to mark another line of dirt on his cheek. He does it over the scar he got from the gunman who shot him. The dirt covers up the scar or at least makes it less noticeable.

He quits clowning around, wads up his shoulder harness, puts it and his weapons in his pants pocket, lifts out the grate, and hoists me out onto the street the way he lifted me out of the wrecked limo.

I straighten up and look around. Alexei climbs out after me and puts the grate back before he takes my hand and we head off walking down the street.

I can't stop staring at everything and everyone. "This is the most surreal experience of my life," I murmur under my breath.

"Why is that?" he asks on the side.

"This is the first time in my life I've gone outside into the city disguised as a regular civilian. This is the first time I've ever gone out without a security escort."

"I am your security escort, sweetheart."

"You know what I mean. No one knows who I am."

"That's the general idea. This is the building."

He leads me into a normal apartment building on the corner. We step into a dark, dingy doorway leading to a tiny, cramped, concrete stairway rising to the second floor.

The carpet on the upstairs floor looks a hundred years old. The wallpaper hangs off the walls and a bare lightbulb dangles by its exposed wires from the ceiling.

"Ugh! What is this place?" I gasp.

"This is the safe house. You didn't think you were going to be staying in a five-star hotel, did you?"

"No, but.....this is a flea pit."

"That's exactly why no one will look for you here. This is the apartment."

He bends down, pulls back the carpet, and lifts a tile from the floor. Someone has broken the tile out of its grout. He takes a key from a hollow underneath and uses it to unlock one of the nearby apartments—not the one next to the broken tile.

He shows me into a grungy apartment with a tiny galley kitchen, a living room the size of my bathroom at the palace, and a single bedroom with one narrow single bed in it.

Whoever decorated this place crammed too many couches and chairs into the microscopic living room. All the furniture leaves only a few inches of space for anyone to wedge their knees between the couch and the coffee table.

A tiny channel of clear floor leads to the bedroom. Other than that, the apartment seems quiet enough.

The one living room window looks out on the side of the building next door. A few feet of space between the buildings let daylight enter the apartment. That's it.

This is hardly a living space. It's more of a closet. In fact, it's less than a closet. My closet at the palace is bigger and much more comfortable.

I sit down on the couch and wilt under the weight of exhaustion. Alexei goes to look out the window and then searches the apartment to make sure we're alone before he comes to sit down next to me.

He peers deep into my eyes. "Are you okay? You should probably lie down and get some rest. You look exhausted, too."

"I am, but I can't calm down. I felt like this after the mall shooting. I could barely move, but I couldn't relax. It took me days before I started to feel normal again."

He strokes my hair and then rubs my back with his big, comforting hands. "You look much better this time. You were borderline hysterical at the country house. This is much more serious and you're handling yourself so much better. I'm proud of you."

I look up at him and our eyes meet. I want him so bad, but I can't take that step. Maybe these clothes play a trick on my mind. I don't think I'm attractive like this—not the way I was in my bra and panties. I looked hot like that.

He pushes against my shoulder. "Lie down, sweetheart. We aren't going anywhere for a while."

He steers me to lie down on the couch, goes into the bedroom, and comes back with a rough wool Army blanket.

He drapes it over me and tucks me in. The blanket is scratchy, but my clothes protect me from it.

He sits down next to me and takes out his phone. "I'm going to call Christophe and then I'll think about getting some food delivered."

I can't answer. Of course he's thinking like that. He always thinks of everything to take care of me.

He taps on his phone screen and holds the phone to his ear while it rings. Christophe answers. I only hear Alexei's side of the conversation.

"Yeah," he clips. "We just got here. Yeah, no problem—I mean it was no problem once we got out of the palace. The intruders were all still there hunting around for anyone still there. Yeah, we made it out in the end, though." He looks over at me. "Yeah, she's fine. She's just exhausted. She's getting some rest. How do we order food to be delivered here? Do you have someone trustworthy you can call—or who I can call?"

Christophe talks for a while and then they both say goodbye and hang up. He puts his phone away. "He wants us to stay here for a while—at least until the security team is certain it's safe to come back. He's going to order some food to be delivered to us. He has someone lined up."

I can't answer. I can't even open my eyes. I drift off and fall into a dead sleep. The last thing I feel is his hand rubbing the side of my arm.

He feels so comforting and reassuring. He's right here next to me. I'm okay as long as he's still here.

Chapter 21: Alexei

I stand by the apartment window and look out at a tiny alley between this building and the next. Whoever selected this apartment as the Royal Family's safe house really knew what they were doing.

No one can access this window or the one window in the bedroom. Someone would have to climb a five-story concrete wall. No one can shoot at this window from the next building, either. The other windows are all too far away.

I glance back toward the couch and wind up staring at Simone. I keep telling myself I shouldn't have touched her and made out with her both in the palace and in the tunnels.

I can't bring myself to regret it, though. She's intoxicatingly sweet. I would give anything to protect her—and I guess that's what I'm doing.

She makes my blood boil. I want her like I've never wanted any woman I've ever met, but I can't have her.

I don't just want her *because* I can't have her. I can't get enough of her. I ache to hold her and comfort her. I love how she gives herself to me. She kisses so fully. She doesn't try to control the situation.

Her screams of ecstasy in the tunnel echo in my ears. I want to hear her like that again. I want to feel her quaking in my arms and know those screams belong only to me.

I want to fill her with so much pleasure and happiness. I want to give her everything, but she already has everything. She has everything I can't possibly give her. I have nothing to give her anyway—except my life.

Someone knocks on the apartment door just then. That must be the grocery delivery.

I draw my sidearms, flatten myself against the wall, and swing the door open. Gunfire doesn't erupt out there.

I stay behind the wall and keep my weapon raised while I squat down, pull the box of groceries into the room, and then shut the door without exposing myself just in case someone is out there.

I straighten up, holster my weapons, and pick up the box. The noise rouses Simone. She sits up rubbing her eyes and sniffing. "What's happening?" she croaks.

"Christophe sent us some groceries to keep us going." I put the box on the coffee table and push the blanket out of the way so I can sit down.

She helps by pulling the blanket to the other end of the couch. She looks adorable in her big, baggy hoodie and wooly hat. I would dress her like this all the time if I was her stylist.

Actually, no, I wouldn't. She looks nothing like her fashion-icon princess image. That's why we're here—to keep her hidden.

Her normal image makes her as visible and recognizable as possible. That's the point of her whole brand.

I rummage in the box and pull out a brown paper bag full of Chinese food. The rest of the stuff in this box is mostly staples.

I push the box away and start dividing the food between me and Simone. She gets up, goes to the bathroom, and then stops off in the kitchen.

She comes back with two plates, two forks, two spoons, and a handful of paper napkins.

"Thank you," I tell her.

"Thank *you,*" she husks.

I look up at her. "What's wrong with your voice? You sound like you're coming down with something."

"I guess I screamed too much at the palace," she croaks. "I think I strained my voice."

I laugh. "You sound like Dame Edna."

She smirks at me. "As long as you don't say I look like her."

"In that outfit? No, you don't."

Now it's her turn to laugh. I dump crispy chicken, broccoli beef, and egg fu young onto her plate, serve myself, and we both start eating.

I lean back against the cushions. She swivels sideways and bends one knee on the cushion so she can face me from the side. "What are we supposed to do here?" she husks.

"Do? How do you mean?"

"Like.....are we just supposed to sit around cruising the internet and wait to hear that it's safe to go back to the palace?"

I look down at her body. "You don't have a phone, do you?"

She makes a face. "How could I carry a phone in that dress? I had to leave it in my apartment."

"That's good. I would have to destroy it so the attackers didn't use it to track you."

Her head shoots up. "They would do that?"

"Of course. They know you survived the assault on the dining room. They saw us running around the palace. They could be canvasing the city to see if you made it out alive."

"So....how long do I have to stay here?"

"I don't know. I'm sure we'll find a way to occupy ourselves. What do you usually do in your free time?"

She raises her eyebrows. "Free time? What free time?"

"Well, you can't always be running around doing public appearances, can you? You go home sometimes. You have free time then."

"I usually have to stay on top of my social media accounts, reply to comments, answer fan mail—all of that."

I frown at her. "So....you don't have any outside interests?"

"My public image is my outside interest."

"I mean something you do for you—something that's only for you—something you don't do for everyone else—something that makes you happy—that improves the quality of your life."

She looks away. Sweet Jesus! What kind of can of worms did I just open this time?

I eat in silence for a while. What am I going to do with this woman?

I pay attention to my food so I don't make her more uncomfortable than she already is.

"What about you?" she finally croaks. "Do you have any outside interests—I mean apart from stroking and cleaning your guns?"

I burst out laughing again. She's really funny. "I used to do logic puzzles when I had to travel for work. Valiyev traveled a lot and I always traveled with him. I used to do logic puzzles on long plane rides and long waits at the airport. I had a lot of time to do that while I was guarding him."

"How could you work on a logic puzzle and guard him at the same time? Didn't you have to keep an eye on the surroundings?"

"Of course. I would read the puzzle, put it away, and think about it while I kept an eye on the surroundings."

She looks down at her plate. "You're smart. I should do something like that."

"You should find something that interests you. You don't have to copy me."

"So will you work on logic puzzles here?"

"I have been. I look them up online. I've been thinking about them while you've been asleep."

"Teach me about one of them."

I put my plate on the coffee table, pull out my phone, and open my web browser. I already have the page open on one of my tabs. I point at the screen.

She leans in close to my head so she can look over my shoulder. "Oh, it's Sudoku. I know what that is."

"Not quite. See how the grid has no numbers in any of the squares to get you started? This is Difference Sudoku. See those numbers on the lines? That number tells you the difference between the two squares on either side of the line. So that number is a six. So the two squares on either side have to have a difference of six. That means one of them could be a nine, a three, an eight, a two, a seven, or a one."

"How is that supposed to help you figure out the puzzle? That's almost all the numbers. If two squares had a one between them, it would be all but one of the numbers."

"That's what you have to figure out. See this square here? It has an eight between them. That tells you that one square on one side has to be a nine and the other square has to be a one. You have to compare the different combinations of numbers and figure out the rest of the grid."

She looks up at me from inches away from my face. "You know how to solve that?"

"Sure. I do it all the time. I'm getting pretty good at it."

"How do you do it? Show me."

She turns back to the phone. I start working out the puzzle, but at that moment, she rests her head on my shoulder and scoots close to me on the couch.

I freeze. She's trying to get close to me again.

I shouldn't go there, now that we're out of danger.

She sits up after only a few seconds, pulls off the wooly hat, runs her fingers through her hair, and settles back down on my shoulder where she can cuddle into my neck.

I should stop this right now—but she isn't doing anything. She just sits near me and leans against me from the side.

I push her up and turn my head so I can look at her. "Listen to me, sweetheart. We need to get straight about what we did in the tunnels."

Her eyes widen with so much emotion. I already know everything she's thinking and feeling—because I'm thinking and feeling the same thing.

"What about it?" she croaks.

"I meant what I said in the hospital. Nothing can happen between us. You know that. I'm a member of staff—and you don't want to get saddled with someone like me anyway. You need to get with someone who is going to stick around for a while."

Her features tremble. "Are you not going to stick around for a while?"

"You know what I mean. My job is dangerous. I already got shot twice—and that's just since I've been working for your family. Anyway, it doesn't matter because I'm sure your father has someone already lined up for you—someone who isn't me."

Her cheek spasms and her mouth twists up in misery, but she still doesn't let herself cry. "I can't stand the thought of anything happening to you!" she chokes. "Thinking about losing you—it only makes me want you even more!"

"I know, sweetheart. I feel the same way about you." I lean in and kiss her, but I make sure to kiss her on the forehead. "You know it could never work. It would be better if we never did anything again. You understand that, right?"

She nods fast, but she won't stop grimacing in misery. She makes no effort to hide how much pain she's in.

"We did it because we both thought we were going to die," I go on. "We were in life-threatening danger. We aren't now. We can think clearly—and we'll probably both make it back to the palace in one piece. We need to pull it back to the way it was before—where you're my client and I'm your bodyguard and that's all."

She nods again and looks away. She tries more than once to speak and fails each time.

Seeing her like this twists my heart. She's so upset about this—about the fact that we'll never be together.

She feels the same way about me that I feel about her, but there's nothing I can do about that.

I pull her into my arms, lean back on the couch, and ease her down on my chest. I kiss her hair and stroke her head. "We're all right," I murmur. "We're here and we made it. We don't have to worry about anything anymore."

She nods against my chest and slips her arms around me. She squeezes me close and then settles down to relax.

I rub her back and shoulders in between running my fingers through her hair. We're together—as together as we'll ever be—just in this moment. That's all we'll ever have.

Chapter 22:
Simone

I scrape the last of my Chinese food into my mouth, suck the sauce off my fingers, and push my plate onto the coffee table before I take a look in the box of groceries and supplies Christophe sent to me and Alexei in the safe house.

He also sent Alexei a charger for his phone so they can keep in touch while we're out here.

"Did Christophe say what was happening at the palace?" I ask.

"He didn't say exactly and I didn't ask," Alexei replies from the window. He sits sideways against the edge of the couch so he can look out. "He said not to come back before he tells us it's safe—which I take to mean it isn't safe—which I take to mean the intruders are still in control of at least part of the building. The security team must be trying to drive them out or capture them."

"How safe are we here?" I ask.

"We're as safe as we're ever going to be anywhere, I'd say—apart from flying to Indonesia or somewhere like that."

"So can I take off this bulletproof vest now?"

"Oh, yeah. I forgot you were wearing it. You can take it off."

I stand up, pull off my hoodie, and start tearing apart the Velcro straps on the vest. The Velcro is really strong. I have to pull really hard.

I finally take the vest off and lay it on the table. I'm only wearing my bra underneath. "I guess I won't be wearing any other clothes as long as I'm here."

Alexei doesn't answer. I look up to find him staring at me across the room. His eyes go hard the way they did in the tunnel—right before he made out with me.

His gaze ranges all over me—all over the part he can see. My baggy pants hang low around my hips. He can see my stomach and the lacy top of my panties.

He catches me watching him and turns back to the window, but it's too late. His feelings didn't just magically change when we came to this safe house.

I pull my hoodie back on and take the groceries and dirty dishes to the kitchen. I put the food away and then wash the dishes. This apartment isn't the greatest, but it could be a lot worse.

Now I have nothing to occupy myself. I go back into the living room, kick off my sneakers, and sit crosslegged on the couch. I'm a lot more comfortable like this.

"Would you mind if I used your phone to get on the internet?" I ask.

"You can as long as you don't log into any of your social media accounts. I don't want the attackers to see that you're alive somewhere."

I wilt. "What would I do on the internet if I didn't log into any of my social media accounts?"

"Try doing some of my logic puzzles."

"No way. That requires too much thought."

He laughs. "That's the idea, sweetheart."

I glance over at him. He still sits with his back to the room. "What are you looking for out there? It's just a blank wall."

"There's an alley down there. Someone might come from that direction—and it's the only place where I can keep an eye on the outside world. It's force of habit—and we aren't completely out of danger here. I can't patrol the building, so watching out the window is the next best thing."

I don't want to work on logic puzzles. I don't want to get on the internet at all if I can't check my social media accounts, so I stretch out on the couch again.

The sun is going down. It will be nighttime soon. I shouldn't be this tired, but I guess I am.

I'm not ready to go into the other room to go to bed yet. I don't know what I should do with myself instead.

He comes over to me, hands me his phone, and says, "Here. Read this."

He puts the phone in my hands and turns the screen toward me. It's already turned on to an e-book reader.

The story is a murder mystery psychological thriller with a strong, male detective from the big city working with a team of local small-town cops after the detective gets stranded in the town when his rental car breaks down.

The story is super interesting and very well written. It draws me in.

I scoot up the cushions, prop my head on the couch arm, and sink into another world. The book is a page-turner. I get completely engrossed in the characters, their interactions, the mystery, and everything else about the story.

Alexei doesn't say anything to interrupt me. I read for three hours straight before I get too tired. I roll onto my side and rest the phone on the cushion next to my head, but my eyes eventually get too tired. I start to shut them and wind up drifting off.

I wake up hours later in the middle of the night. It's dark, but a faint glow of city light shines through the living room window.

I wake up when Alexei picks me up off the couch, cradles me in his arms, and carries me into the bedroom next door.

I'm still half-asleep. Feeling him next to me feels too good. I hug him around his neck and rest my head against his shoulder while he lowers me onto the bed.

I start to sink back into sleep. I don't realize what's happening until he takes hold of my hoodie and starts tugging it up to take it off.

I'm too drowsy to think too much about that. He pulls the hoodie over my head and throws it on the floor. I'm more comfortable without it.

He unbuttons my pants and pulls them off, too, before he draws down the covers for me to get into bed. I snuggle between the sheets. I'm much more comfortable here.

My eyes barely drift open to see where he is. I expect him to leave me alone to sleep in the bedroom while he sleeps on the couch or something.

He surprises me by pulling off his shirt and climbing into the bed with me. He slides down between the sheets, draws the bedding over both of us, and wraps his arms around me hug me close.

I stare at him in the dim light for a second and then sink into the blissful warmth of his skin. He feels dreamy like this.

He rolls onto his side facing me and holds me the way he did in the tunnel. I can accept one night of just lying here holding him. It's enough.

Everything changes when he pushes me back and looks into my eyes. He looks at me the way he did in the tunnel—and then he kisses me.

It isn't the tender, protective kiss that tells me we're both better off if we keep away from each other.

This is the ravenous, animalistic, aggressive kiss that tells me everything he's capable of. This is the kiss from when he pinned me against the wall and made me scream.

His hands start to explore my body as our breath strains between our mouths and the tension mounts in both of us.

His fingers flex into my hip in an unmistakable grabbing motion. He creeps down and crushes my ass in one firm hand while he steers my hips into his movements.

I gasp and then he eases off slightly. He stops kissing me and holds eye contact with me while he unclips my bra.

I can't stop staring at him as that sensation sparks and fizzes all over my skin. He's undressing me. He's lying shirtless in bed with me. He must plan to really do this.

He turns me on like I can't believe. I want him so bad I can't stand it. His eyes drive me wild as his warm fingers slide my bra straps down my arms and he pulls my bra away to leave me exposed.

He burrows down inside the bed, flattens one hand against my back, and inhales my breasts into his mouth. I whimper in ecstasy when he devours them in greedy mouthfuls.

He slides his knee between my legs and then seizes my ass to crush me down on his leg. His hands guide me in a maddening rhythm to spiral me out into space.

I hug his head against my chest. He's all over my breasts—sucking, kneading, pinching, teasing.

I whimper in his ear. Something tells me it wouldn't be a good idea for me to dissolve in screaming orgasm here. The neighbors would hear and ask questions.

I have to be quiet, but he doesn't make it easy. I can't stop moaning when his fingers creep around my ass getting closer to my slit.

I rock harder on his leg. He leans back and lets me see all the smoldering ferocity in those eyes. His arms, chest, and shoulders strain with muscle each time he flexes them to pull me into that rhythm.

I gasp and moan with each pump of my hips. Now he can see how much I want this—how much I need this.

He doesn't look away. He plays with my breasts to turn me on while I cycle higher into the stratosphere.

Without warning, he shoves his hand into my panties and stabs two fingers inside me on the next stroke. I wind up pumping all the way down on them.

I barely stop myself from screaming out when a blast of cruel desire courses through me. He's doing it. He's taking me.

I burst into a reeling climax, but I can't let myself scream. I ride down on his hand whining and sobbing in miserable delight. I drift off into the clouds, but he doesn't let me look away.

He grabs the back of my head, clenches his fist in my hair, and pries my head up. "Look at me!" he snarls. "Look at me!"

My eyes snap wide open. I can't look away from his ferocious glare even as I groan and convulse in the throes of a brutal climax.

"Come on!" he murmurs. "Come on! That's right."

His voice intoxicates me with his power, but I'm already starting to come down from that peak. I start to drift into a hazy dream of bliss.

He pulls back, slides his fingers out, and rolls me onto my back. I flop down on the bed in exhausted bliss, but he isn't finished yet.

He sits up just enough to slide my panties down. Is this really happening? Is he really doing this?

He confirms it when he lies back down on his back, unbuckles his belt, and pushes off his pants and shorts. We're both naked and lying in bed together.

I stare at him in shocked amazement when he turns over to face me. He sets his features in a solid mask of iron will. He's going to do this. He wants it. This is our one night together—one night out of a lifetime.

He props himself on his elbow, kisses me, and his fingers find their way to my swollen flesh again. He excites me more than I can stand.

I moan again when he circles his flat fingertips against my clitoris to wind up back up to the pinnacle of ecstasy. I cling to him for dear life, but he silences me with his mouth.

The rasping, animal husk of his breath tells me how much he aches for this. I can't stand the fierce determination in his eyes. He trains all his powerful will on me. He wants me and he's going to take me.

I writhe in front of him as he works me into a frenzy. I don't look away from his eyes even once. He sees me surrendering to everything he does. I'm his for the taking.

My own movements cause me to accidentally brush my hand against his solid slab of meat between his legs. I somehow lost awareness that it was there.

I grasp it without thinking and his nostrils flare in a sudden gasp of pleasure when my fingers close around it. He stares at me even more fiercely, but now I see how much he wants this, too.

I stroke him a little harder and a little faster. His features strain. His lips fall open as the sensation stretches him to the breaking point.

Each breath escapes him in a little husky gasp between his bared teeth. I want to make him explode in my hand.

His shaft bulges and the veins distend between my fingers even as he rubs me into a frenzy of my own. I'm getting closer to the breaking point. Is he going to climax with me from touching each other?

He rolls over onto his stomach and flexes his hips to pump into my hand. That movement sends me reeling into another soul-destroying climax. I want him to take me. I want him pumping into me like this.

He doesn't stop. He growls under his breath each time he thrusts into my hand. He gasps at the deepest point of his stroke. His body feels so strong and male and primally intense.

I can't stop what's happening to me. I clamp my eyes shut as the wave thunders over me, but I have to keep looking into his eyes. I have to make him see.

He rolls the rest of the way on top of me without asking or suggesting anything. He doesn't try to pull out of my hand. He just moves over between my legs and lets me steer him into my waiting channel.

My hand falls away and I rock in a sea of delight as his thickness finds its natural path all the way home.

Now I can wrap my legs around him, bury my face in his neck, and feel him moving inside me, building up power, and carrying me out of this world into an endless sky full of stars.

Chapter 23: Alexei

I lie on my back with my arms around Simone. Her head rests on my chest. Her arms wrap around my ribs.

She keeps running her fingers over me and tracing her fingers around my scars. I have a lot of them from all the gunshot wounds and surgeries I've had in my career.

"We can never do this again," I murmur into her hair. "You understand that, right?"

She nods. "I know. I just don't want to lose you."

"You won't lose me. I'm still here."

"But for how long? Something could happen to you."

I shut my eyes against her hair. "You know it's the same for me, don't you? Every day I live with the nightmare that something might happen to you. All these people are trying to get to you. It kills me."

She squinches her head farther down into the hollow next to my heart. She keeps pressing her ear against my sternum to listen to my heartbeat.

I love that about her. This isn't about sex for her—just like it isn't about sex for me.

"That's twice you've taken a bullet for me," she murmurs. "How can I live with that—knowing one of these times might kill you? I don't want to go anywhere or do anything or see anyone if it's going to put you in danger."

I hug her tighter. "You have to. You have responsibilities."

"I don't have as many responsibilities as that. I won't do it if it puts you at risk. It isn't worth it if I might lose you—and for what—so the public can see what I'm wearing today? It's stupid."

I pull away and push her back to look into her eyes. I can't believe I'm hearing this from her.

"What are you actually saying?" I ask. "Are you saying.....?"

I don't say it. Her eyes overflow with emotion.

Is she saying she would cut back on all her appointments and appearances—to protect me? Is this thing really going as far as that?

God knows why I even ask that when I feel the same way about her. I would take a bullet for her. I already have and I would do it again—and not because it's my job.

I can't lose her. I would rather see her get with another man and live happily ever after. At least she would be safe. That's all I care about.

I care about a hell of a lot more than that. Looking into her eyes tells me more than I could ever learn by talking to her.

Her heart, her care, her inner goodness—I want her for myself. I want to feel how much it hurts her that I might get hurt.

Her heart is so pure. I want that heart only for myself. I want her to care about me as much as she can and for me to care about her as much as I can.

No amount of telling myself it's impossible will ever change that. I want her even if I can never have her. I want to love her. I want to show her what it would be like for a man to love her for who she is—not as some fancy princess.

It's still dark outside, but I don't know what time it is when my phone rings across the room. I plugged it into the charger before I got into bed with her.

I have to pry myself out of her arms and cross the room to get the phone. The screen says it's quarter to five in the morning. Simone and I have been up all night enjoying each other's delights.

The call is from Christophe. "How is everything?" he asks.

"Everything is fine. Thank you for the supplies."

"I want you to leave the safe house, Alexei," he tells me.

"Is the palace secure?"

"No, it isn't. That's exactly why I want you to leave. I want you to take Simone to another, secure location outside of town in the country. I'll send you directions—and I'll send you directions to a secure underground garage in town where you'll be able to get a car. The garage has a concierge who will give you the keys. Take Simone and leave town. We're still looking into who's behind this. We aren't sure if they're out in the city looking for you."

"Are you…..are you all fighting in the palace? I don't like leaving you in danger."

"We aren't fighting in the palace. We're all under lockdown while the Army clears the intruders from the palace. You can't help us and you would have to leave Simone in danger if you came back. I'm ordering you to take her out of town. You'll go to Château des Gennennois. It's an estate in the countryside. You'll be able to protect Simone better there. I don't want you to stay in the safe house longer than you have to and we have no way of knowing how long the siege will last."

"Okay. If you say so."

"How is Simone?"

"She's fine. She's much better now that she isn't so scared."

"That's excellent. I'm sure she's in the best hands with you. Make sure she understands that the whole family is safe and well."

"I'll tell her."

We hang up and I stare at the phone for a long time. I really don't like leaving in the middle of a major battle.

I wouldn't be able to help the Army get the intruders out, but it seems wrong to take Simone away in the opposite direction from the rest of the family.

"What did he say?" she asks from the bed.

I take the phone with me when I sit down on the bed next to her and then slide back under the covers.

"He wants me to take you to Château des Gennennois. No one knows when the Army will secure the palace. He doesn't want us to stay here when no one knows if the attackers have people searching the city for us. He says you'll be safer out in the countryside."

She eases close to me and her arms surround me again. She sinks lower onto my chest. "I'm relieved. I'm not ready to let you go yet."

I kiss her hair and fold her in my arms. I'll never be ready to let her go, but I'll have to eventually.

The inevitable moment when this bliss ends—it makes the time so much sweeter because it can't last.

I don't know how long I'll be able to spend with her, but I plan to savor every minute while I have the chance. I don't want to miss even one second of feeling her near me.

I want to kiss her and ravish her body the way I did last night, but we're both too tired. We sink into an exhausted sleep with this feeling lulling us into a dream world.

I wake up a few hours later when my phone buzzes. I rub the sleep out of my eyes so I can focus on the screen.

I find two messages from Christophe. The first is directions to Château des Gennennois. The other is all the information on the garage and the car I'm supposed to drive to get there.

Château des Gennennois is a long way out of town in the mountains. Remote countryside surrounds the estate and it has its own security team. Christophe is also sending in additional personnel in readiness for me to bring Simone there.

The place also has its own housekeeping staff. Simone will be a lot more comfortable there for as long as the siege lasts. We won't have to run the risk of ordering groceries from someone who might tell someone else where we are.

She's still asleep in bed when I get up, put on my pants, and go out to the kitchen to make her breakfast.

She seems so much more normal now. She doesn't act like an entitled princess. She's just a young woman like any other—the vulnerable young woman I've been watching over all this time.

She likes to relax on the couch with a good book. She likes talking to her friends and admirers. She isn't so different from every other young woman her age.

I don't know why I thought it would be any different, but she doesn't act like royalty. She's just a person like any other.

That makes her feel so much more accessible. I adore her like this. She's over there asleep in the bed we shared last night. She moans when I touch her and when I move inside her. She responds when I kiss her.

She's all the woman I need and she's beautiful from the inside out.

She's just starting to stir when I take her breakfast into the bedroom and sit down on the mattress next to her. "Take a shower after you eat," I tell her. "You can wear the same clothes and change when we get there. Make sure you put on that bulletproof vest under your hoodie."

She rolls over and her eyes float open to meet mine. "What about you?"

"Well, we only have one vest and you're the client under protection here, so you have to wear it. If everything goes the way it should, we won't meet anyone before we get in the car and drive out of town. Now come on and get up. I don't want to hang around here any longer than we have to."

She sits up and starts eating the food I gave her. I try not to notice her naked body when the sheets fall down her chest. Her hair is a mess and she looks all rumpled without her makeup on.

I go back out to the living room and stay there to eat my breakfast while she takes a shower and gets dressed.

I check all the directions and touch base with Christophe's concierge about getting the keys to the car once we make it to the garage. He says he'll meet me there. He better or we're going to have a problem.

Simone comes out of the bedroom wearing her old clothes. Her hair is wet and messily finger-combed.

She pulls her hat over her head and sits down across from me. "When are we going?"

"As soon as I wash up." I go into the kitchen, finish the dishes, and put all the groceries back into the box they came in.

"Why are you bringing that?" she asks. "The staff will feed us as much food as we want once we get to the estate."

"I'm bringing it for this." I stick both my shoulder sidearms and the holster inside the box. "I can't wear them or carry them in public without giving myself away. If the shit hits the fan, I'll drop the box and grab my guns." I give her a look. "You grab the guns, too, if anything happens. Understand? Be ready to defend yourself."

She looks down at the box. "I don't know how."

"I'm sure you'll figure it out. Let's go."

Chapter 24: Simone

Alexei picks up the box containing our remaining groceries and his weapons. He opens the apartment door, steals a look outside in both directions, and nods his head to me to tell me to follow him.

We take the stairs back to ground level. He keeps hiding behind every corner and checking the area outside before he goes out into the open.

I stay behind him and flatten myself to the walls when he does. I don't know what he sees out there.

I want to hold his hand, but he has to carry the box in both of his. I finally can't stand the tension anymore, so I hold onto his belt instead.

We make it as far as the open street before he stops again. "We're going out there now, so try to act as casual as possible," he murmurs. "Just look straight in front of you. Don't glance around like you think someone is following you. Understand?"

I nod. I'm not sure if I can do that, but I have to at least try. He answers all my prayers by transferring the box under his left arm and taking my hand in his right. Thank God for that.

We walk out into the street. I look straight ahead and don't glance around. I'm too freaked out by the way he's acting.

I can't tell if he's looking around. He must have a way to check his surroundings without giving too much away.

He strides down the street at a brisk but normal pace. No one would think he was rushing.

I see us from an outside perspective. I look like a dumpy teenager who hasn't gotten the memo on how to dress. He looks like some workman carrying a box of groceries and leading his insecure girlfriend along by the hand.

We don't look like anything special. A few people greet Alexei and say good morning to him. He replies easily and even smiles at a few people. He never stops walking.

He turns a corner, passes down another avenue, and turns again to a much larger street where he enters an office building full of people in business suits.

We look completely out of place here, but no one pays any attention. We cross the lobby and enter the stairwell. We're finally alone.

I feel Alexei straining with the tension. He acts so casual and put together on the outside when he's really wired to the limit on the inside.

I catch a glimpse inside the box. His two guns sit on top of the groceries where he can grab them at a moment's notice.

Would I be able to use those guns to actually shoot at another living person? I don't know about that—but what if something happened to Alexei?

I get a flashback of that moment when I found him shot in the face on my patio. I don't want to go through that again, especially not now that he means so much more to me.

What if he got shot right in front of me? I would pick up a gun to protect him. I don't know if I would be able to protect him or even hit anything, but I would do it.

He wears another smaller revolver on the back of his belt. He leaves his T-shirt untucked to cover up the cross-draw holster.

He carries two other guns strapped to each of his ankles. He always comes prepared. I have to be prepared, too. I have to be ready to grab any of those guns if he needs me to.

The office building stairs lead down into an underground parking garage full of cars. We climb down four levels and the garage still keeps going down.

Alexei leads the way to one of the rows of parked cars. They all look the same.

He stops next to a Mercedes roadster where a man in a tailored business suit stands there waiting for us.

"Emil?" Alexei asks.

"Yes, indeed. Here you go." Emil pulls a set of car keys out of his pocket and bows to me. "Your Highness....it's always a privilege to serve the Royal Family."

He walks off without another word and leaves me and Alexei alone with the car.

Alexei unlocks the car, opens the passenger door for me to get in, and puts the grocery box on the back seat before he gets behind the wheel.

He turns the ignition and starts the motor, but he doesn't leave until he pulls on his shoulder holster and holsters both his guns.

"Does the staff at the estate have access to other stuff?" he asks while he buckles his seatbelt.

"What do you mean by other stuff?"

"I need to reload when we get out there. I need them to get me some ammunition. Do they have someone like that they can send out to get supplies?"

"Oh, yes. You can ask Arnaud. He's the butler at the estate. He can get you anything you want."

He nods at nothing, compresses his lips, and looks around in all directions before he puts the car in gear. He reverses out of the space, drives through the garage, and roars out onto the street.

He sets off driving fast through town. The engine rumbles and the car hums all around me. Alexei keeps shooting fierce glances on every side of the car and into the rearview mirror.

He finally motors onto the highway and drops the pedal all the way down. The car shoots away into the countryside.

I can finally relax here. We're leaving all our problems behind. We aren't really, but driving away from them sure does feel good.

I take my hat off, rake my hair back, and recline in the seat with a sigh. Alexei smiles over at me and then squeezes my hand. He looks and acts much more relaxed now, too.

The countryside falls away on either side of the car. The city disappears and we curve around mountains putting more and more miles between us and the palace.

He finally turns into the driveway at the estate. Tall oak trees surround the entrance and line the driveway all the way up the chateau.

The staff comes out to meet us when he parks in front of the house. The butler rushes over and pumps Alexei's hand. "It's so good of you to bring Princess Simone to us safe and sound, Sir. My name is Arnaud. Please let me know if I can do anything to assist you."

"I need you to get me a hundred rounds of .44 caliber hollow-point bullets and a hundred rounds of .35 caliber of the same—as soon as humanly possible—and I need you to tell me everything you know about the security situation at the estate," Alexei replies.

"Of course, Sir. We'll get onto that right away. You and Princess Simone must come inside, change your clothes, get comfortable, and I will send Sebastian to see you. Prince Christophe put Sebastian in charge of security until you came. I'm sure Sebastian will be anxious to hand off to you and hear from you how you would like the men to guard the estate." He turns to me. "Please follow me, Your Highness. I can only imagine the ordeal you've been going through."

Alexei and I exchange glances on our way inside. Neither of us looks like we belong here in our filthy, oversized, grungy clothes.

Alexei wears his sidearms right out in plain view in front of the staff. No one comments on them or our appearance.

One of the underbutlers brings in our box of groceries, hands the phone charger to Arnaud, and takes the box away to the kitchen.

Arnaud leads us upstairs and shows me and Alexei into rooms right next to each other. "Please make yourselves at home," Arnaud tells us. "You can ring the bell if you need anything at all. I will send Sebastian up in half an hour to see you, Sir. Will that be soon enough?"

"That will be fine," Alexei replies. "Thank you."

Arnaud bows and the servants leave. I cast one last glance at Alexei before we both go into our rooms.

I shut the door and sink into an armchair by the big windows leading out to my balcony. This room is much more luxurious and ornately decorated than my apartment at the palace.

I'm finally safe. I feel bruised and skittish after everything that's happened, but I made it thanks to Alexei.

The servants have left the room full of clothes my size. I can take the hottest bath of my life, wash my hair, and change whenever I want to, but I don't do it right away.

Care and agitation weigh me down. It's going to take me some time to relax after everything I've just gone through—and it isn't even over.

Alexei is still preparing for the next bad thing that happens. He's getting ready and coordinating with the other security guys in case someone comes to the estate.

I wish I could spend time with him alone here without all the servants and security people around, but maybe I'll be able to, now that we're away from my family.

I won't be able to spend time with him dressed like this. I hunt through the closets, select the outfit I want to wear, and go into the bathroom.

The staff has also brought in all the hair and makeup products I need to start looking like a princess again.

I stand in front of the mirror and stare at myself for a long time. I don't look like a princess. I look like a plain, boring, ordinary, normal young woman with no special skills, abilities, or education—because I don't have any.

Alexei still likes me this way. He likes me without all those clothes and makeup. He spent the night with me when I was at my lowest point.

None of those things exist between us. Whatever this is between us goes deeper than that.

That moment has passed, now that we're back around people who treat me like royalty. Arnaud and the other servants will treat Alexei as my bodyguard—because he is. That's all he'll ever be.

I strip off all my old clothes, take a long bath, and then rinse off and wash my hair in the shower.

I put on my usual clothes. I recognize quite a few of these outfits from Lucille's wardrobe. They're all clothes I've worn before. They fit and I feel comfortable dressed like this.

I throw out the bra and panties I wore to the dinner and afterward. The lingerie set is filthy after wearing it for three days. I never want to see that set again as long as I live.

I hesitate to get rid of the hoodie, hat, baggy pants, and sneakers, though. I want to keep them to remind me of my time with Alexei.

I fold up the clothes into a pile, put the sneakers on top, and stash everything in the bottom drawer of the dresser. I'll decide what to do about those clothes when the time comes for me to return to the palace.

I do my hair and makeup before I leave the room. Alexei's bedroom door stands open. He isn't in there anymore. Of course not. He won't let any grass grow under his feet as long as any security threat endangers the Royal Family.

I go downstairs and find Arnaud setting the table in the dining room. He sets out a place for one. "Where's Alexei?" I ask. "He should be eating lunch, too."

"He already ate in the kitchen, Your Highness. He's already gone out with the other security guards."

I gape at him. "He ate in the kitchen?! Why?"

He frowns at me. "He's a member of staff, Your Highness. He eats with the rest of the staff."

I shut my mouth with difficulty. I should have thought of this. I did think of it. Why did I think it would be any different after we came back?

I will never share those moments with Alexei again. That window closes behind me.

I sit down and Arnaud serves me a big feast of pasta, salad, crusty homemade bread, seafood canapes, and a bowl of ice cream afterward. Did Alexei get the same meal? I bet he didn't.

I want to go look for him, but I can't do that. He's already back at work without a single hour break.

I don't have anything else to do at the chateau. I should go up to my room and catch up on sleep.

Alexei's warning comes back to me. I could ask Arnaud for a new phone, but I don't want to log into any of my social media accounts until Alexei and Christophe tell me it's safe.

I don't even want the temptation of having a phone. I don't want to do anything that could heighten the security risk.

I go up to my room, but I don't go back to sleep. I wander around at loose ends for a while and then wind up staring out the window.

As soon as I get there, I spot Alexei down in the grounds with a bunch of other security guards.

Alexei is wearing a suit again. Christophe must have sent that out for him, too—or maybe Christophe told Arnaud to get it.

Alexei will be wearing his sidearms under that suit. He wouldn't go out to work without being fully armed and ready for anything.

Alexei stops there on the grass, points in different directions to send the guards to different parts of the estate, and then takes three of them with him when he strides out of sight.

I'm safe right now because of him. He risked it all to get me out of the palace. Now he's out there making sure I'm still safe even here.

What the hell has my life been all this time without him? How did I not see before how much I needed someone like him?

I don't need *someone* like him. I need *him*. I don't need anyone else. It has to be him.

That can never happen. I can't even indicate to any of the other servants that I'm interested in Alexei. He would lose his job if anyone found out.

One night. We had one night. That's all we'll ever have. He's been telling me that since we left the palace and he's right. My heart just hasn't caught up with the rest of me yet.

He isn't here for me to look at anymore—or for me to talk to or cuddle up with. He isn't here to explain his logic puzzles to me.

My being revolts that I have to let go of him. Every ounce of my soul tells me to go with him and stay with him.

That will never happen. He's a bodyguard and he'll stay a bodyguard. He won't step out of line.

He'll keep working for the Royal Family until some threat tries to kill one of us. Then he'll do his job and get killed in our place—probably in my place.

I'll have to let go of him then, but I don't want to. I don't want to let go of him ever.

Chapter 25: Alexei

Someone knocks on my door. I'm still staying in the upstairs bedroom of the Château des Gennennois—the bedroom next to Simone's.

This bedroom is way too luxurious for me. It looks like it was decorated for some dignitary or head of state.

I've already asked Arnaud to move me down to the servants' quarters, but he says Christophe wants me to stay next to Simone's room just in case.

The room makes me uncomfortable. I don't want to spend time in here, but I guess I have to.

I go over to the window and squint out at the grounds. The estate covers a hundred acres of countryside in all directions. The other guards run regular patrols around the grounds. I'm in charge of them so I don't have to go.

I can see for miles in every direction from this window. It's a magnificent view—just like everything at the Château des Gennennois is magnificent.

This room is magnificent. The whole house is magnificent. The sunshine glows on the hills.

I'm just deciding what to do with the rest of my day when someone knocks on the bedroom door. I answer it and find Simone standing there.

She looks the way she did at the palace with her hair and makeup impeccably done up. She wears tight, charcoal-grey capri pants, tiny sneakers, and a flared pink blouse with a dark blue blazer over it.

She bursts into a huge grin when she sees me. "Hi!" she chirps.

"Hi. What's up? You look really nice."

She blushes. "You're back in suit mode, I see." She waves me out of the room. "Come on. We're going out."

I raise my eyebrows. "Out? Out where? We aren't supposed to leave the estate."

Her eyes twinkle when she laughs. "I don't mean out like that. I'm going for a walk in the grounds and you're supposed to come with me."

"Oh. I see." I step out of the room and shut the door behind me. "You're settling in, aren't you? Everyone here is so nice."

"Arnaud is like the grandfather we never had. Seriously, if you need anything, you only have to ask."

"I know. He got my ammunition in record time. I swear he must have had it on the premises. He wouldn't have had time to go get it."

"Maybe he got it from the other security guards."

I look up at her and then look away. "Oh, right. Of course."

We go downstairs and she opens the big front doors for me to go outside with her. "What have you been doing since we got here?" she asks.

"Mostly just checking the place out and taking the handoff from Sebastian to manage the estate's security. There isn't a lot else to do."

"At least you have something to do. I don't have anything."

"You need a hobby. Maybe one of the housekeepers could teach you how to knit."

She bursts out laughing and blushes at me. "Stop it."

"What's wrong? That will keep you off the internet."

She won't stop giggling. "I'm sure my fans would have a field day if I started knitting at press conferences and fashion expos."

"You could start a new trend. Tom Daly did it by knitting next to the Olympic diving pool. If it's good enough for him, it should be good enough for anyone."

She laughs again as we cross the big lawns to enter the grounds. We walk around the first stand of trees and she slips her hand into mine.

I jump away and take my hand out of hers. "What are you doing?! Are you trying to get me fired?"

"No one can see us. I want to spend time with you."

"You are spending time with me."

She takes a step closer. "You know what I mean."

"We agreed we wouldn't."

She rises on her tiptoes and kisses me on the lips. "You can't blame me if I find you irresistible."

She walks off following the garden paths. I have to catch up with her. "You're flirting with disaster, you know," I tell her.

She beams at me and slips her hand into mine again. "I'm just flirting with you, sailor."

Now I'm the one who blushes. Walking through the grounds holding hands with her sure does feel good. I don't want to stop.

We keep walking farther and farther away from the chateau. She's right. We're completely hidden here.

I take a chance, push her into the trees, and back her up to one of the trunks while I kiss her to the ends of the earth. Don't ask me how I'm going to survive this when we get back to the palace.

She wraps her arms around my neck and then moans when I lift her thighs to pull her legs around me.

I grind between her legs, but I don't let myself take it any further than that. I wish I could. I wish I could nail her right here. I shouldn't even be going this far.

"Come into my room tonight," she whispers between kisses. "Or let me come into yours."

"We shouldn't....." I have to break off when I kiss her again. I can't get enough of her.

"I need you!" she whimpers. "I don't want to stay away from you. I'll be quiet. I swear."

I feel my body starting to take over, but it's more than that.

Her suggestion makes me stand up and pay attention. I shouldn't spend the night with her here, but I already know I will. I need her just as much. I need every minute with her that I can get.

The urgency of our time on the run somehow keeps going here. All the conversations we keep having about something happening to one of us—that doesn't change, now that we're here.

It will never change. I need to feel her near me every second I can get for the rest of my life.

She'll die eventually. Even if I got lucky enough to spend the rest of my life with her, she would still die eventually—or I would.

I need to grasp every one of those moments. I need to experience all of her in my life all the time—but I can't.

I put her down and take her hand again. We walk through the woods, but we walk together like a couple instead of client and bodyguard.

My mind goes into a tailspin. I'm already over the edge with her. I can't come back from this. She already has my heart.

How did I let this happen? When did it start? Did it start at the country house? Did it start during the limo crash? Did it start the first time I took a bullet for her?

It's too late for me now. I'm already in over my head.

We walk a long way—much farther than we should. We have to let go of each other's hands when we come upon some of the guard patrols, but Simone and I always rejoin each other's hands as soon as we pass out of sight.

I finally escort her back to the house and upstairs to her room. She grabs my wrist, pulls me into her room, and pushes me against the shut door as soon as we get inside.

"Spend the night with me," she whispers.

"You come to my room," I whisper back. "You can move around more quietly than I can."

"I want to have breakfast with you afterward. I want to spend the weekend with you."

I laugh and straighten up to look down at her. God, she means so much to me! I don't even know how much she means to me.

"We aren't on a country holiday here, you know," I tell her.

She smirks and kisses me one last time. "What time should I come tonight?"

"Whenever you think it's safe. The servants won't question you walking around in the middle of the night—not like they would if they bumped into me."

She kisses me and opens the door. "Okay. I'll see you then."

I go back out into the hall and return to my room. Am I really going to do this? It sure looks like it.

I shut my door and go over to the window with my head in a whirl. I'm going to spend another night with Simone. Will it continue like this once we get back to the palace?

I shouldn't be doing this. I shouldn't sneak around behind her family's back when there's no chance in hell that she and I could ever get together.

That doesn't seem to matter anymore. Something tells me we're already together. We're as together as we can possibly be.

It would be a black stain on my career if I got busted doing it with a client behind closed doors—a client's daughter. That would be worse, but it wouldn't be the end of the world.

Is she worth it? Hell yes. She's worth it for the way she makes me feel. She makes me feel like we could actually have something real if not for her standing.

My phone rings just then. It's Christophe.

"We finally got the intruders rounded up and shipped off to the slammer," he tells me.

"Who are they?" I ask. "Is it Blood Tide?"

"We don't know who they are until the authorities identify them and communicate with Interpol about their past records. Anyway, the palace is secure now. You and Simone can spend the night there and come home in the morning."

Those words set off a rocket in my mind. *Spend the night.* I'm going to spend the night with Simone. Just one night.

I thought that about last night. Now we're doing it again. Where will it end?

"How are things looking out there?" he asks.

"All quiet. We aren't seeing anything. I don't think the attackers planned for anyone to make it out this far. Sebastian and his men are really thorough. They had the place locked down before Simone and I got here. We should use him and his team again in the future. He's the best I've seen since I came to work for you."

"Good. We need people like that. Maybe you can tell him before you leave to contact us at the palace. We'll bring them in as soon as you come back."

"Great. I'll see you tomorrow."

I hang up and stare down at my phone. He has no idea I'll be spending tonight with his sister. He would fire me for sure if he knew.

Chapter 26: Simone

I press my ear to my bedroom door to listen, but nothing moves in the rest of the house. Of course it doesn't. It's eleven o'clock at night.

Arnaud and the other servants usually go to bed around nine—or they at least retire to their rooms then. The house falls silent.

None of the servants come up to this part of the house at this time of night—not unless one of the guests rings the bell for something.

I ease the door open, listen again, and dart down the hall to the next door. I have to be careful when I open it. The doors in the chateau creak and squeak sometimes.

I dart inside and shut the door behind me before Alexei attacks me from out of the darkness. He's wearing a T-shirt and sweatpants.

I'm wearing my flimsy cotton pajamas. This is the closest we can get without being naked together.

He pushes me back against the door and mauls my mouth with hungry kisses. I kiss him back with all my might. This is our last night together. I have to feel and experience everything with him before morning separates us.

He plasters me against the door, pins my arms above my head, and grinds into me, but he turns me backward just as fast.

He tears down my pajama pants and drills into me from behind while he holds my wrists together against the wall above my head.

I want him to attack me. I want him to ravish me. I want him to get as aggressive as he wants to—just for one night.

I whimper under my breath as the energy spirals off the charts, but I have to keep quiet. No one can find out what we're doing.

He doesn't go easy on me. He pumps into me with wicked, masterful strokes and launches me into a mind-blowing climax unlike anything I've ever known. His power and energy take over my body so I have no choice but to respond.

I'm still reeling in delirium from that when he pulls out, turns me around, and hitches my legs up around my waist. He leans me back against the wall and drives into me from below while I sway and undulate in his arms.

I swim in a sea of ecstasy when I stare into his haunted eyes. All the passion and desire between us throbs back and forth from his soul to mine when he looks at me like that.

I keep drifting into these fogs of rapture. I climax again and again without stopping. How is he doing this to me?

He carries me to the bed and we fall into the same wild torrent of positions, pleasures, and shades of emotion sweeping through us.

I see all his tenderness, all his burning animal passion, and all his power written in his face. He rolls onto his back and sits me up on his lap to ride him into infinity. He turns me over onto all fours on the mattress to make me his plaything.

Everything he does conquers my heart and makes me crumble into his hands. The sky is already starting to get light by the time we both collapse in exhaustion.

I buckle onto the bed next to him, but I can't fall asleep. I keep my eyes open for one last long look at him lying spent and magnificent on the bed.

His body breathes with so much masculine beauty. He lies across the bed like a god in an ancient painting. He's the perfection of manhood, inside and out.

My fingertips trace the clefts of his muscles as the daylight creeps over him. I'll carry all these secrets with me when we go back to the palace. Arnaud told me yesterday that Christophe is recalling me and Alexei to town.

I'm ready. I'll hold Alexei in my heart after this, no matter what.

I roll up onto my hands and knees. His hand closes around my breast in one last squeeze when I kiss him.

Then I slip away, grab my pajamas, and run back to my room. I already hear the servants moving around downstairs.

I get straight into the shower and get dressed before I go downstairs. I want to leave the biggest possible delay between when I come downstairs and when Alexei comes down.

I'm eating in the dining room when I hear him talking to Arnaud and Sebastian in the entrance foyer. Alexei doesn't come into the dining room. He goes to the kitchen to eat breakfast there.

I eat slowly and calmly. This calm penetrates all the way down to my soul.

I'm ready to go back to the palace even if it means Alexei and I will never spend another night together again—never kiss again—never hold hands again—never look at each other like that again.

I carry this experience in the secret corners of my heart. I carry *him* in the secret corners of my heart.

He said I would never lose him and now I know it's true. He would always be there—always cherishing me—even if I married someone else.

He comes in half an hour later and asks if I'm ready to go. I say yes.

We go out to the driveway where the servants put my suitcase into the roadster's trunk. I packed my hoodie, wooly hat, baggy pants, and sneakers into the suitcase yesterday. I'm taking them home with me.

I'll never wear them again. They represent the greatest night of my life—the greatest love of my life. No one will take Alexei's place after this.

I can live with that now. I feel that with rock-solid certainty.

The servants all wish me well and assure me they're ready to serve me anytime I come back. I thank them all and Alexei opens my door so I can get in the car.

We don't talk on the way home. He drives one-handed so we can hold hands instead. One car ride out of eternity. We can hold hands this once before the end.

We let go when he pulls into the palace limo entrance where the Royal Family always gets into and out of cars. Security guards surround the car.

Alexei gives me one last look before the guards escort me inside. I lose sight of him, but he'll still be around.

He'll go straight back to taking care of security. That's his job. I'll see him as my bodyguard whenever I go anywhere in public. He's still out there guarding me and making sure I'm safe even when I can't see him.

I walk into a scene of mass chaos. The servants work all over the palace to clean up the mess. Workman rope off sections of the walls to plaster up all the bullet holes, sweep away debris, and repair the floors, doors, and furniture.

The palace doesn't look like a palace. It looks like a disaster zone. Some of the floor sections still have white tape outlines in the shape of fallen bodies. Police cordon tape blocks off whole rooms—including the dining room.

I meet up with my family and hug everyone. They won't stop talking about how they got out of the building once the siege started.

They all want to know how Alexei and I made it out. I tell the whole story, but of course I leave out the parts where we made out and spent the night together.

I eventually break away and go to my apartment. I fall into another few hours of dazed stupor when I realize I'm finally home and safe. My family is all right. We're putting the pieces back together.

The servants bring in my suitcase. I'm just unzipping it when Christophe comes to see me. He hugs me and stands there with his arm behind my back. He beams down at me with so much love and gratitude. "Thank God you made it!"

"I'm okay. It was touch and go getting out of the palace, but we made it. I was just worried about all of you."

"How did Alexei do it?" he asks. "What happened to you after the shooting started in the dining room?"

"I told you. He saw those men pulling their guns. He tackled me before the first shots went off. He pulled me under the table and then we ran out the back of the dining room once the battle got closer to the outer corridor."

He raises his eyebrows and sits down on the couch. "It's hard to imagine we all made it out alive. The attackers infiltrated the catering company. They did it weeks ago—even before we started screening their employees. We're going to have to get much tighter on security after this."

"That reminds me." I sit down in front of him. "I want to cut back my social schedule—like radically cut it back. I might even do away with it altogether."

His jaw drops. "You don't have to do that. We can find a way to mitigate the risks so another situation like the mall doesn't happen."

"No, I want to. I'm certain. I don't want to keep making these appearances. You can work it out with Chevalier. I'm sure I can continue my social media presence and interact with the public in other ways. The security concerns are too great."

"I'm surprised to hear you say that. You were so committed to it before."

"That was before—before all of this." I go back to my suitcase and touch the Notre Dame hoodie, but I don't take it out. I don't want to show it to Christophe. "A lot of things changed since this whole thing started."

He stands up. "Well, I'm delighted to hear that you finally understand the danger you were putting yourself in. I'm sure cutting back your schedule will be fine. We'll find other ways for you to continue your social presence." He heads for the door. "I'll see you down at dinner tonight. We're all looking forward to welcoming you back."

He leaves. Now I can finally move my baggy old clothes to the bottom drawer of my dresser. They'll stay there forever.

I unpack the rest of my things and turn on my phone so I can finally go on social media. I announce to the world that I'm back at the palace.

I do a short video post in the sunshine on the patio outside my apartment. I tap on the phone to post the announcement and say a few words about the siege. That's all. I don't have to put myself at risk to let everyone see me.

I sit back and enjoy the sunshine after that. I'm much more content with this life and my decision than I thought I would be.

Christophe thinks I'm worried about my safety. I'm more concerned about Alexei's safety. He's the one who would be in more danger if I went out. I can't let that happen.

I might never get to be with him again, but at least he'll be safe.

Chapter 27:
Alexei

I point to a layout of the palace grounds. "This is where the intruder jumped the wall and snuck up to Princess Simone's patio. The secondary patrols will canvas these shops on the other side of the street. Sebastian's men will wear plain clothes and keep an eye on the wall from the outside. They'll be able to see if anyone tries to get over the wall. Then our people will radio the guard patrols on the inside to intercept the intruder as soon as they get inside."

"What about guards inside the palace?" Pascal asks me.

I point to different spots on the floor plan of the palace itself. "We have regular posts here, here, and here. The patrols go through these central corridors on a regular rotation. They'll make side runs into the lesser-used parts of the palace, but not as often. You and your brothers should announce at dinner tonight that we'll be sending guards into everyone's apartments at least once a day to search for any threats. Each of you will be able to designate a time when you can vacate your apartments for the search. We won't conduct them when anyone wants privacy."

"I'm sure it won't be a problem," Dorian tells me. "We already discussed it with my uncle while we were locked down during the siege."

"Perfect. I just want to make sure he understands why we have to do this."

"He understands," Salvatore tells me. "He insists that you take all measures you think are necessary."

I'm just bending over the grounds layout again when Christophe comes in. He looks over our shoulders and joins me, Pascal, Renáld, Dorian, Salvatore, Casim, and Sebastian at the table.

"In the future, the team and I will be making routine searches and assessments of all venues outside the palace where any of the Royal Family makes an appearance," I tell them. "We won't leave security to the venue itself. That will be stipulated in any contracts or agreements beforehand. We'll have unrestricted access to the venue before and during the event for the purpose of assessing and carrying out security measures."

"By the way, Alexei," Christophe interjects, "Simone just told me she plans to radically curtail her public appearance schedule. She finally understands that the risks are too great. She'll continue her social presence from the palace and reduce her appearances to the bare minimum."

I only nod. "Good. That's one less thing we have to worry about. Her schedule was starting to give me nightmares."

The others laugh. "She won't be able to get out of making an appearance at the Prince of Luxembourg's birthday party," Renáld points out. "That's coming up at the end of the week—and I doubt the Prince's security team will let us take priority over them."

"We'll work together with them," I reply. "Who's going to the party?"

"Just Simone," Christophe tells me. "He invited her personally. He would probably be offended if she canceled by saying his security wasn't good enough to protect her."

"Some appearances will be necessary. We won't be able to eliminate all of them and we can vastly improve the ones she still does. We could have avoided the mall situation if we only took reasonable precautions." I shake that out of my head. "Never mind. We don't need to dredge up the past."

"So what do you want to do about the Prince's birthday party?" Christophe asks.

"I'll get in touch with his security team and explain that I want to go over their protocols before Princess Simone attends. I'm sure they'll be happy to walk me through their procedures." I straighten up. "I'll talk to her about the changes we'll be making to her routine. I'm sure she'll be accommodating."

"You're the only one she'll be accommodating to," Dorian tells me. "You tamed the wild tiger at last."

"Hardly. She's perfectly reasonable."

"Only with you," Salvatore tells me.

I turn away from the table. I don't want to talk to them about Simone. "I'll catch up with all of you later. Let me know if anything comes up."

I get out of the security office as quickly as possible and head down to the residential wing. I would be seeing Simone about her security arrangements anyway. I'm not doing anything outside my job description here.

I knock on her door and she calls, "Come in!" from inside.

I walk in and find her sitting in her living room tapping on her new phone. She smiles and gets to her feet when she sees who it is.

"Back at the grindstone already, I see," I tell her.

She makes a face and puts her phone on the coffee table. "It's a full-time job. To what do I owe the pleasure of this visit?"

"Christophe told me about your decision to cut back your schedule." I study her a little closer. "You did that for me, didn't you?"

"Of course I did!" Her features tremble. "I told you I would. Did you really think I would deliberately put you in danger?" She loses the fight to control herself. "Everything that happened at the mall and afterward....it was all my fault....."

I cross the room in a heartbeat and wrap my arms around her. I can't even kiss her.

My heart breaks that I'm holding her so close like this and I can't even do that. She's completely out of my reach even when she's leaning right here against me.

"Don't beat yourself up about it," I murmur into her hair. "We have each other because of what happened at the mall. Come on. Don't cry."

She straightens up and looks up at me through brimming eyes. "Promise me you won't take any unnecessary risks, okay?" Her voice breaks. "I'm serious. Promise me you'll be careful."

"I am being careful. I'm always careful, but I do have a job to do. It will never be completely risk-free."

"I know that." She wipes a tear off her cheek and then grimaces. "I just don't want anything to happen to you."

I kiss her on the forehead and rub her back. The feelings between us have already spiraled so far beyond what I realized.

I feel the same way about her. I feel much more compelled to be careful so nothing happens to me, now that I know I have her. I don't have her and yet I do. I have her in every way that counts.

"We need to talk about the Prince of Luxembourg's birthday party."

She huffs and throws herself down in her chair. "I don't care about the birthday party. We can cancel it for all I care."

"Christophe says the Prince invited you personally. Christophe says the Prince would be offended if you backed out by implying that his security isn't good enough. It sounds like you have to go."

"Do whatever you have to do with the security. I'll take whatever precautions you want me to take up to and including canceling my attendance. I'm sure you have plenty of ideas about how I can attend safely—or as safely as possible—and you'll be there, won't you?"

"Of course. I'll be acting as your bodyguard."

"That's good enough for me. If the security arrangements aren't good enough for you, then I just won't go. The Prince can be as offended as he wants to be. It doesn't mean anything."

"It means something. I'm sure there will be a lot of these events and appearances that you can't cancel."

"You told me a dozen ways we could have prevented the whole mall disaster. Just do your assessment, make your decisions, and I'll abide by them. I have no desire to see you or me get hurt."

"Okay. I'll handle it." I sit in the chair next to her and take her hand. "Are you going to be okay?"

"I'll be okay as long as you're okay."

I stand up, but I can't even speak to take my leave from her. I kiss her on the head and walk out of the apartment.

I care about her more than I can stand, but we can never be together. This is a far worse disaster than if the Royal Family found out and fired me. Now what am I supposed to do?

Chapter 28:
Simone

I keep my hand on Alexei's arm while we glide through the Prince of Luxembourg's party. "How long do I have to stay here before I can make a fashionable exit?" I ask under my breath. "We've already been here for two hours."

"You understand these things better than I do. Why don't you tell him you're still fragile from the siege and you need to go home and lie down—or tell him you have a headache?"

I laugh. "That's to get out of sex, silly. He would take it to mean I was interested in him."

He stretches his neck and squints over the crowd. "He's standing over there surrounded by ten other girls. I think you should just slip out the back and disappear into the night. He'll never know the difference."

"That would be rude."

"Then tell him you have another public appearance scheduled for tomorrow and you need to make arrangements for that. Tell you had a lovely evening and maybe you can catch up another time."

I find myself blushing at him. "You should be my public relations manager. You could put Chevalier out of a job."

"No, thank you. Come on. I'll drag you over there kicking and screaming if you don't come willingly."

I laugh again. I've been talking to almost no one other than Alexei all evening. Everyone else here is too busy talking to each other.

I see these events so differently now. My heart just isn't in them. I can't count the minutes fast enough before I can go back to the palace and forget all about these people.

Alexei stands off to one side watching while I make my excuses to the Prince. Then Alexei and I get into the limo to go back to the palace.

I pull him into my apartment and sway in his arms kissing him before we say good night. "Are you sure you can't spend the night?" I ask.

"What will you do if I say yes?"

I laugh, but I have to do it quietly. "I'll cry myself to sleep and then pleasure myself for hours fantasizing about you."

Now it's his turn to blush. "Stop it. Don't tease me."

"I'm not teasing." I take his hand and pull him toward my bedroom. "I want you. Spend the night with me."

He sinks on top of me on the bed and then has to get up a second time to shut the bedroom door.

We take our clothes off and dive under the covers together.

I wake up alone the next morning, look around, and groan when I see the clock. It's already eight-thirty. Alexei must have gone to work a long time ago.

He can't afford to get caught in my bedroom. He must have slipped out and gone back to his own room before anyone else in the house woke up.

Will it be like this all the time—him guarding me by day and us sneaking around to spend the night together behind closed doors? This isn't what I want with him.

I drag myself out of bed at nine, take a shower, get dressed, and eat breakfast in my apartment. I need to retool my social media schedule, now that I'm doing so many fewer appearances.

I get on my phone, log into my daily planner, and start shuffling things around. I get halfway through it before I get another knock on my door.

I look up, but the door opens before I can say anything. My jaw drops when Sebastian and five of his men walk in without waiting to be invited. They all come armed and they keep looking around like they expect the worst.

"Would you please come with us, Your Highness?" Sebastian asks.

"Where are we going?" I ask.

"We need to move you to another part of the palace. We have some issues with our security that we need to take care of. We're taking precautions with the Royal Family's safety just in case."

They start leading me out of the room. "Where's Alexei?" I ask. "He's the one who usually guards me."

"He's in another part of the palace dealing with the threat. I'm sure he'll catch up with the family after it passes."

They take me out of my apartment and escort me down the hall. I can't help but look back over my shoulder. Is Alexei in danger right now? Is he out there getting shot at? Is that the security threat he's dealing with?

How did this happen? How can he be in danger already when I just went to so much trouble to protect him?

The security guys lead me to a fortified room in the palace. My whole family is already in there. The guards steer me inside and shut the doors. Christophe, Dorian, and Salvatore lock the doors from the inside. No one can get in or out.

"What's going on?" I ask as soon as they finish.

"We got a report from one of Sebastian's men that another intruder tried to get over the wall into the grounds," Casim tells me. "The guards have been searching the grounds for the person, but no one can find anything."

"Where's Alexei?" I ask. "Is he out there, too?"

"We don't know," Pascal tells me. "We only heard about the report from the guards when they came to get us. They didn't give us the details."

That only makes me more agitated. The safe room isn't big enough for me to pace around in—not with the whole family crammed in here.

I wind up in a corner turning one direction and then the other. I can only pace from one corner wall to another.

Why does no one know where Alexei is? Why hasn't anyone told us what's really going on out there?

He better not be hurt. I can't stand that—not now when I'm actually starting to have real feelings for him.

He said we were together. He said we were together because of what happened at the mall.

Why can't we be together? Who made up this stupid rule that no one on the staff is allowed to get involved with anyone from the Royal Family?

That rule is as old as the Royal Family itself. I'm sure plenty of princes from generations past had their flings with the palace chambermaids. They never got involved or got serious. The princes certainly never married any of those chambermaids.

I can't keep still. One hour passes another. The time drags at an excruciating pace. Why doesn't someone come to get us? How long can this go on?

The guards don't come back for another five hours. I'm wearing a hole in the carpet when my mother, Aunt Marguerite, and Emeline come over to me.

"Everything will be all right, darling," my mother tells me. "The guards won't let us out until they make sure it's safe."

"She's on her last nerve after all the recent attacks," Marguerite remarks on the side.

Emeline squeezes my arm. "We all understand. We're all scared. It's okay."

I try to wave them away. None of them understands because they don't know about Alexei.

Geneviève sits right over there on the couch next to Christophe. Neither of them has to worry about the person they love going into danger. Same with my parents.

This is my worst nightmare—that something will happen to Alexei. What if another siege breaks out? What if he gets shot again? How am I supposed to live like this?

We both tried to prevent it by not getting involved. Now that horse has left the barn. We are involved. We're as involved as we can possibly be.

One of the guards calls Christophe's phone from outside the safe room. He and my cousins unlock the door. "Thank God!" my mother breathes.

The others stand up and gather around the doors to finally get out of here. We get mobbed by an even bigger group of guards who hustle us back to our residential wing.

"What's happening?" Christophe asks them.

"Get down the tunnel—NOW!!" Sebastian orders. "Go! Go! Get out of the palace!"

I try to turn around. "Where's Alexei?"

The guards completely ignore me. I feel my nerves snap while I wait for Christophe and the others to lift out the floor of the cleaner's closet. This brings back too many memories of escaping with Alexei.

My brothers push my parents and all the rest of us down the stairs. Sebastian hands Christophe a flashlight and then lowers the floor back into place.

"This way!" Christophe clicks on the flashlight and leads the way back to the safe house.

Dorian, Salvatore, and Casim boost my father and all the women out onto the street first. My brothers and cousins climb out next. It's already nine o'clock at night. The street is deserted.

My world crumbles on the way up the stairs to the safe house. We all have to crowd inside. There isn't enough space for all of us to wait in the living room.

Marguerite, Johanne, Emeline, and Daphne go into the bedroom. The rest of us mill around in the living room.

This apartment floods me with memories. Alexei—he must be dead by now. He would have been the one to come and get us—not those guards. He would have made sure we got out of the palace in one piece.

I can't keep still. I can't even sit down. I pace back and forth from the kitchen to the one part of the living room with no one crowded into it.

My cousins come over to me next. "It's all right," Salvatore tells me. "We're safe here for now. The security guards would have told us if we were in danger of another attack."

I can't even accept my family's assurance. They think I'm scared of the danger.

I turn away and wind up looking into the bedroom. My sister, cousins, and aunt sit on the bed where Alexei and I spent the night.

My brothers and father sit on the couch where Alexei and I shared that Chinese food.

None of these people knows what's really bothering me. I can never tell them. I can never confide in a single living soul that I actually met and fell in love with the man of my dreams.

I love him. I want him in my life. I even want to marry him—and I can't. I may have already lost him. I *have* already lost him because I never had him in the first place.

Chapter 29: Simone

I jump out of my skin when someone touches my arm. I spin around and find Pascal at my side.

His eyes look into the deepest, darkest depths of my soul. Can he see the truth written there—that I'm in love with Alexei?

"We just got the call," Pascal tells me. "We're going back to the palace."

I barely understand what he's talking about. My family has been hiding out in the safe house for two days. I'm a nervous wreck about leaving, but I'll lose my mind completely if I don't find out what's happening with Alexei.

I can't even outright ask Christophe to ask Sebastian and the other guards if Alexei is all right. That would give too much away.

Pascal's eyes overflow with sympathy and concern. My whole family looks at me like that now. They don't understand why I'm so jumpy and agitated when we've been safe here all this time.

I practically disintegrate in nerves when the security team comes to get us. They load us all into limos and take us back to the palace.

Everyone else goes to their apartments to change their clothes and catch up on sleep in comfortable beds for a change. My mother,

Marguerite, and the other girls have been sharing the one bed in the bedroom.

My father has been sleeping on the couch. My brothers and cousins have been sleeping on the floor.

I haven't slept at all. My nerves are completely shot, but I can't even sit down to relax.

I pace through the palace looking in every room. I even look in Alexei's room in the servant's quarters. He isn't in there.

I question all the servants. None of them can tell me anything. The security guards don't stick around long enough to answer my dozens of questions.

He can't be dead. Why won't anyone tell me either way? What are they waiting for? Why is everyone staying so secretive about what happened to him?

No one would have to keep it a secret if he was all right. I'm going out of my mind. I can't even think straight anymore.

I'm making my third circuit of the palace when Christophe comes up to me. I don't even stop walking. He has to fall in next to me. "Come down to the other end of the palace. I want to talk to you in my apartment."

"Why?" I ask over my shoulder. "I'm a little busy right now."

"What are you busy with?" He studies me extra closely. "The palace is secure. You don't have to worry about anything. The security team wouldn't have brought us back if it wasn't safe."

I wave him away. "We'll have to talk later."

He doesn't hesitate. He takes hold of my elbow a lot more firmly than I expect. He doesn't try to make me stop walking. He steers me into one of the parlors I just happen to be passing at that moment.

"Hey!" I try to struggle out of his grip.

He pushes the door shut behind him and it slams. He doesn't let go of my arm. He pulls me into a chair and twists my arm to make sure I stay there.

"Did you hear what I said?" he snaps. "We're back in the palace. We aren't in danger. You can settle down. You're worrying the whole family with your behavior."

I start to stand up. "That isn't important. I have to go find out if...."

He plants his hand on my shoulder and shoves me back down in the chair. He shoves me down hard. "You aren't going anywhere. You've been driving yourself insane for three whole days. Now tell me what the problem is. You were out of your mind in the safe room and you didn't even sleep in the safe house even though I heard Salvatore telling you we weren't in danger. Your mental state only seems to be deteriorating here even though I just told you the palace was secure. What is wrong? Why are you so worked up?"

I stare up at him trying in every possible way to think about what he just said.

I can't think about anything other than Alexei. He's out there somewhere and he's in danger if he isn't already dead.

I open my mouth to make some excuse—some flimsy little nonsense lie that will get me out of this room.

Getting out of this room won't tell me where Alexei is or if he's in the hospital fighting for his life or if he's already dead.

Christophe lowers his voice and his whole tone softens when he sees me struggling to speak. "What?" he murmurs. "What's wrong?"

"Alexei......" I can't say it. I can't even ask.

He frowns. "What about him? Don't worry about the state reception at the end of the month. Some of our other men will guard you...."

"I don't want anyone else guarding me!" I hear my voice rising. "Where's Alexei? What happened to him?"

"He's busy dealing with all the threats against us. You know that. If you have a problem with these other guards...."

"I don't want another guard, Christophe!" My voice breaks into a shriek. "You have to bring him back!"

His features harden. "Alexei has other duties besides guarding you. You knew this when we brought him on. We always said we wanted to hire someone who could manage our entire security operation. We were always going to move him out of guarding you so he could focus on the bigger picture. If you have some reason to think these guards aren't adequate, you better tell me now. Otherwise, you'll have to be satisfied with them."

I can't take it anymore. I can't take the strain of not knowing where he is. I look away, and without meaning to, I completely break down in tears.

This has been coming for three days. Actually it's been coming for even longer—since I first started to care about Alexei.

Christophe steps closer, drops on one knee, and squeezes my hand. "Hey! What's going on with you? This can't be about the guards."

"Alexei...." Saying his name makes me break down crying even harder. "You don't understand, Christophe!"

"We all admire Alexei," he murmurs. "He's more than any of us thought he could...."

"You don't understand! I love him! I fell in love with him!"

A dangerous silence falls over him when I say those words.

"He's everything I always wanted in a man....and now I love him......we spent all that time together......at the safe house and the es tate.....and we can never be together......and now he's out there.....and I don't even know if he's alive or dead....."

I can't take it anymore. I cover my face and let the sobs pour out of me. I can't live with this secret any longer—not if it means I can't even ask where Alexei is or if he's alive.

Christophe's hand goes cold on mine. He gets to his feet and stands there staring down at me while I sob my eyes out. I can't even look up at my own brother.

He's technically Alexei's boss—and now I just outed Alexei to Christophe.

Christophe stays silent for so long that I really start to fear the worst. He eventually rests his hand on my shoulder. "I don't know what to say," he husks. "He's such a fine man. We all love him like he was one of us.....I couldn't ask for a better man for you.....I just don't see any way to resolve this."

His kindness and understanding only twists the knife. Now someone knows—someone important.

"Alexei is safe out there," Christophe murmurs. "He's fine. He's in charge of our operations. He isn't dead or even injured—and I promise you he won't suffer from this. I don't know what to do about it, but he'll stay here. I won't tell anyone that I know—except him, of course. He should know that you told me."

He squeezes my shoulder once more before he walks out.

I can't even go back to pacing around looking for Alexei. All my nervous exhaustion crashes down on top of me. I bury my face in my hands and sob my heart out.

I love Alexei, but he might as well be on the moon. He might as well be dead to me. Then I could grieve his loss and move on. Now I can't even do that much.

Chapter 30:
Alexei

I pass one of the guard patrols near the palace perimeter. No one is on the grounds. "I'm going back to the office," I tell the other guards. "Call me if you see anything."

They nod and say, "Yes, Sir." It looks like I'm in charge of palace security now.

I make it halfway there before I meet up with Dorian, Salvatore, and Casim. "What's the situation?" Casim asks me.

"It's all secure. We're falling back to the office."

"What was that about?" Dorian asks me. "Was there an intruder or not?"

"I'm still not sure. Sebastian is questioning the guard who reported someone climbing over the wall. We'll know more once we get those answers."

"What answers could the guy give us?" Salvatore asks. "He saw someone. What more do we need to know?"

I don't answer. I can think of a lot of things the guard might tell us. He might tell us that he's a member of Blood Tide and he reported someone climbing over the wall to get all our security guards out of the palace into the grounds.

That might not be what really happened, but I wouldn't be doing my job if I didn't at least check.

"Did you check the security cameras for an intruder?" Casim asks.

"Don't ask him that!" Salvatore fires back. "Of course he checked the cameras. What do you think—that Christophe just hired someone out of the phone book." Salvatore hesitates and then turns to me. "You checked them, right?"

"Yes, I checked them."

"And?" Casim asks. "Did you see an intruder or not?"

"No, I didn't, but we still need to treat it as a credible threat."

I don't add the other obvious implication of this—that the guard who reported the intruder *is* the threat.

I don't say those words out loud. Dorian, Salvatore, and Casim are members of the Royal Family. They're the Crown Prince's nephews and he treats them as his own sons.

I don't want to alarm them—not until I hear back from Sebastian.

I also don't want to cast suspicion on the guard until I have some reason to. He could have made a genuine mistake or he might really have seen someone climb that wall.

The other possibility is that Blood Tide or whoever is doing this sent someone over the wall to trigger our security measures. Then, when the guards went out to intercept the intruder, he climbed out and ran off.

Whoever these people are could be trying to weaken our system by triggering it with false alarms. Blood Tide will get everyone so frazzled that we slacken our vigilance. Then they'll strike.

We make it halfway back to the palace before we see Christophe, Pascal, and Renáld coming toward us. I'm starting to feel attached to all these men. They're all strong, protective, and their honor is unimpeachable.

I really got lucky when I came to work here. I can't remember ever feeling this connected to any client.

They're Simone's family, though. They'll never accept me. Even one of them finding out what I did would mean the end of this happy arrangement.

"It's almost dinnertime," Christophe tells everyone when they come up to us. "All of you should go inside and start getting ready."

Pascal, Renáld, and their cousins continue on to the house. Christophe and I go with them for a little way before he lays his hand on my arm to stop me. "Hold on a second, man."

I stop and turn to face him. "Is anything wrong?"

"No, not at all.....except that Simone is really worried about you. It seems that no one told her where you were or what you were doing since the initial warning went out. She feared the worst and she's been driving herself crazy all this time because she thought something happened to you."

I stiffen. I don't like where this is going, but he only lowers his voice a little more.

"She told me," he murmurs. "She told me enough. I can't say....I can't say I hate the idea.....I just don't see how anything could ever come of it."

"I know that." I look down at my hands. "I shouldn't have let it happen. I accept whatever decision you make about it."

"The only decision I can make about it is to keep you on. We need you too much and I can see how much she needs you, too. She's.....she's never acted like this about anyone. You're.....you're special to us all. None of us wants to lose you and I wouldn't break my sister's heart by sending you away. You're a good man and we all respect and admire you. I wouldn't choose another man for her, but......there's no way. I'm sorry. I can't lie and say there is."

I can't look up. I stare down at my hands. "I know." My voice breaks. "I swear I will never let this interfere with my work. I'll always give the Royal Family the best I have..."

"I know that, Alexei. I never doubted that." He doesn't say anything for a second before he touches my elbow. "Don't worry. You're safe."

He leaves it at that and we both head off to continue down the lawn. He goes off to the newly restored dining room and I go to the servants' quarters.

That's where I belong because I'm a servant. I'm an employee. I was never going to be anything else to a princess.

I go to my room, shut the door, and slump on the edge of the bed. I look down at my hands in my lap.

Christophe knows. He said I'm safe and he can't think of a better man for his sister, but that means nothing. It's impossible. It's as impossible now as it was in the beginning.

The only difference now is that I love her so much more. She's a piece of my heart walking around another body. How am I supposed to function without her?

I should have ended it at the beginning. I should have ended it before it ever started, but then I wouldn't have her. I wouldn't have her heart right here inside me.

We're together even though we're not. I wouldn't want to give that up. I wouldn't want to give up any of it, not even how much this hurts right now.

I can't see her again—not like that. I can't hold her or kiss her or sneak into her apartment to spend the night with her. I just have to end it now before it ruins what little is left of my life.

This hurts a thousand times worse than getting shot in the chest five times by Valiyev's killers. I would gladly go through that again to escape this agony right now.

I would do it all again, though. I would do it all a hundred times for one kiss from her—one night with her.

She's the only woman I want. She's the only woman I've ever felt this way about—and she's out of reach.

She'll just have to stay that way. We'll go back to being client and guard from now on—for real this time. It's the only way either of us can live with this.

Chapter 31: Simone

I walk into Lucille's fitting room and stop on the threshold. Alexei is already in there going through the clothes on the rack as usual.

He turns around and his eyes brim with painful emotion when he looks at me.

"Hi," I squeak.

"Hello. How are you? Christophe said you were really upset that something might have happened to me."

I open my mouth and try to make some sound come out. "No one would tell me what happened to you.....and I couldn't ask....."

He crosses the room and stands right in front of me. His presence relieves all my tension, but the racking agony of the last week still nags at my gut.

"We can't keep doing this," he murmurs. "You know that, right? It's killing both of us."

Tears spring to my eyes. "I love you!" I choke on the words. "I've always loved you!"

"I love you, too, sweetheart," he whispers. "I love you more than life itself—and that's exactly why we can't do this anymore. You can't keep thinking about me like that and either can I—not when there's no way we can ever be together. We're just hurting ourselves by wanting each other."

I can't answer. He's right. The last week nearly broke me.

He clasps my cheek and bends in to kiss me on the forehead. "Put it aside," he murmurs. "We both have to. It was never going to be. Maybe it was too good to be. I don't know. I do know this is the best thing for both of us. We both need to stop thinking about each other and move forward to whatever happens after this. Can you do that?"

I nod down at the floor. I know he's right. He was right about it from the beginning, but neither of us wanted to listen to that.

"I'll always love you," he whispers. "I'll always hold you in my heart—and I'll never stand in the way of you finding happiness with someone else. I only want what's best for you."

Those words bring the tears to my eyes, but right then, Lucille comes in and starts fussing about Alexei messing with the clothes on the rack.

He backs off, but he doesn't leave. He watches every detail of my wardrobe appointment for the state reception. Then he hovers around the hair stylist and makeup artist as usual.

I sit in the chair in a numb trance. It's over. The intense love and emotion between me and Alexei—it's all over. What we had is gone and will never come back.

I know he'll always do what's best for me. That's exactly why we have to end it.

I would never stand in the way or make trouble if he found happiness with someone else. I want him to.

I want him to find someone who can give him what he needs. I want him to find someone who worries about him as much as I do—someone who can take care of him and be there for him.

That isn't me. I can't be there for him because I'm the focus of this whole thing. I can't give him anything because I don't have anything.

That's me. I'm a princess and I have absolutely nothing to give the one person in the world who means the most to me.

I can't take care of him. I can't even give him my love. How terrible is that?

I don't even pretend to notice when he stands outside the dressing room and evaluates my gown when I come out wearing it. His eyes mean nothing when they follow my curves and discover everything my clothes reveal.

He doesn't get that hungry look in his eyes. He looks only as a professional.

It means nothing for me to I slip my arm into his elbow and have him escort me to the limo. He sits next to me on the seat the way he always does. It means nothing.

It doesn't mean anything for us to walk into the state reception together with me on his arm like he's my date or something. He isn't. He's my bodyguard—that's all.

I make the rounds and socialize with everyone. I meet and greet the other guests. I pass my brothers and cousins in the crowd. Then I stop to pass the time with Marguerite for a while.

My parents stand on the other side of the hall. My father wears his fancy dress uniform covered in medals. My mother looks stunning in a long, regal, purple gown.

Everything will go back to normal after this. This whole thing between me and Alexei will fade away as if it never happened.

My schedule will never go back to the way it was before. I couldn't put any other guard at risk like that even if the guard isn't Alexei.

I'll cooperate with whoever becomes my new bodyguard. Alexei will supervise the security measures of the few appearances I still make. The mall disaster will never happen again.

I'll never let myself get this attached to any security guard again. I'll never let myself get this attached to any member of the staff again.

I'll never let myself get this attached to anyone unless I know there's a real possibility we could wind up together. I can't take this.

"I'm going to go talk to my parents," I tell Alexei. "My face hurts from smiling so much."

He smiles at me and escorts me over to my parents. My father presses Alexei's hand. "This event is going so much better than the others, thanks to all your herculean efforts, my boy."

"It's my privilege, Your Highness," Alexei replies. "The Royal Family's safety is my top priority. I only wish we could have accomplished this sooner without so many issues."

"Things should improve now that you've made these adjustments," my father remarks.

My mother pulls me over next to her. "How are you feeling, darling?" she asks.

I scan the reception. It's as beautiful and luxurious as all these state events. "I seem to have lost my appetite for social occasions like this and all the meaningless small talk that goes with them."

She smiles at me. "I lost my appetite for them long ago. You won't see me running around hosting fashion expos and doing public appearances—not if I can avoid them. I prefer the quiet life."

"How do you do it, Mama?" I ask. "How do you cope with the demands of royal life with so much grace and resilience? I wish I could be like you."

She squeezes my arm. "You are like me, darling. You go through the motions in front of the cameras and then retire to your apartment in the palace where you can be yourself behind closed doors."

"I don't even know what being myself is. I don't know if I even have a self anymore."

"Of course you do," she insists. "Maybe all this commotion clouded it for you just now, but it's still there. I'm certain of it."

I become aware of Alexei listening to our conversation. He would say I have a self, too. That's the part of me he loves, but I don't see it.

I don't even have any personal interests. I don't have anything I do just for myself—something no one knows about. My whole life is geared to be visible to the public.

"Maybe I should take up knitting," I remark.

My mother doesn't answer. She doesn't laugh the way I expect her to. She doesn't even look at me.

I glance over at her to see if my comment offended her in some way.

She stares out at the crowd. Something in the way she stands there doesn't look right. "Mama?" I ask. "Are you all right?"

She doesn't answer. She doesn't turn to me. That's when I realize she isn't blinking, either.

"Mama?!" I ask a little louder. I still get no response, so I wave my hand in front of her face. She still doesn't blink.

Alexei sees something wrong and steps in front of her. "Your Highness? Princess Jasmine?"

My father glances over, and right at that moment, my mother's knees buckle under her. She topples.

Alexei lunges for her, grabs her just in time, and lowers her to the floor to stop her from falling flat on her back. "Your Highness!" he yells in her face.

She doesn't respond at all. Her eyes stare past him in a fixed, glazed, trance.

"Mama!" I throw myself forward, but the crowd realizes something is wrong. Everyone crowds around. I can't even get near my mother.

My father stands there staring in shocked horror. Alexei pulls out his phone and calls an ambulance. I can't even hear what he tells the dispatch operator.

Everyone around us yells, shoves, and tries to get near him and my mother. The shoving, jostling crowd pushes me to one side and I get shunted out of the ring. I can't even see my mother or Alexei anymore.

Security guards swarm the area. Four of them surround me and then dozens more move in to push everyone away.

I scream out when I see Alexei doing CPR on my mother. He gives her mouth-to-mouth and then switches to doing compressions. She lies on the floor with her eyes fixed wide open. She stares up at the ceiling.

The guards start to pull me away. More guards grab all the rest of the Royal Family, drag us outside, and push us into our limos to drive us back to the palace.

I get into a limo with Marguerite, Dorian, Johanne, and my father.

My father sits there in a catatonic stupor all the way back to the palace. Dorian is the only one here with a phone. He calls Christophe and then the hospital.

Dorian gets put on hold and doesn't take the phone away from his ear even when we get out of the cars and go inside.

We meet up in the drawing room down the corridor from the dining room. We always seem to use this drawing room for family emergencies and exceptional circumstances.

Christophe, Dorian, and Salvatore spend the entire time on their phones trying to get some news about my mother.

"Maybe we should just go to the hospital," I tell Emeline. "They would have to tell us what's going on if we just land on their doorstep and refuse to leave."

"We can't go to the hospital without a security escort," she replies. "Alexei would have a fit if we just drove over without even any guards."

She's right, so I shut my mouth and wait. The anxiety of not knowing about my mother starts to wear on everyone—everyone except my father.

He sits on the couch staring in front of him. He almost looks the way my mother did right before she collapsed.

Something in my father's demeanor tells me he's still there. He still blinks and gives very tiny reactions to movement and voices around him.

We wait half an hour before Alexei comes in. He's alone.

He stops on the threshold, casts one pathetic look around, and lowers his eyes to the ground. "I'm sorry...." he husks. "She's gone. She didn't even make it to the hospital. The ambulance crew declared her dead at the scene. The Police took her body to the morgue."

Marguerite screams and Emeline bursts into wild sobs. Christophe's hand flies to his mouth.

My father lowers his eyes to the carpet, too. Marguerite, Johanne, Daphne, Emeline, and Marguerite wrap their arms around each other all sobbing their eyes out.

Pascal and Renáld hug each other. My cousins stand off to one side in stunned silence.

I can't move. I stare at Alexei. Sweat saturates his hair and shirt. He must have done CPR right up until the moment the paramedics told him to stop.

I want to go over there and put my arms around him. He went through something tonight—maybe something even more devastating than anything anyone in this room is going through.

The howling sobs coming from behind me stop me even from taking the first step toward him. I'll never be able to comfort him or to take comfort from him—not ever again.

He looks up, sees me staring at him, and walks out of the room.

He'll spend tonight alone in his room. I'll spend it here with my family while we all try to comprehend this new disaster we all have to find a way to survive.

Chapter 32: Simone

I open my apartment door and listen. I don't hear anyone moving around out there.

The palace is in lockdown ever since my mother's death. We're all in isolation during the mourning period leading up to the official state funeral.

My family doesn't get together for family dinners. I haven't seen anyone since that terrible night when she collapsed right in front of me.

I sneak out of my apartment. I'm not supposed to, but I tiptoe down the hall and ease open the door to my father's apartment.

It's such a cruel blow that he has to stay here alone without the woman he spent his life with. The staff should have at least let him spend the mourning period in another apartment.

I shut the door behind me just as one of the security patrols comes by on their usual rounds. I don't know for certain, but I suppose Alexei is still running the security arrangements behind all of our backs.

He must be planning the funeral and everything since Christophe and the others are all incommunicado.

I sneak through the living room of my father's apartment. He isn't in here. I glance into the bedroom. He isn't in there, either. Did the staff move him after all?

I even check the bathroom and still have no luck. I'm just about to give up when I see him sitting in a chair in the sunshine out on the patio.

My heart lifts. Maybe he isn't as devastated as I thought. I crack the patio door and inch up next to him so I can see his face.

My stomach plummets into my shoes when I see his face. He looks like a corpse except that he's still alive. He looks ten times worse now than he did the night my mother died.

I cringe to think he's been sitting with this alone ever since that night. How could anyone come up with such a heartless custom?

I pull up another chair next to him and lean in close. His eyes don't track my movements. He doesn't see me at all—or does he?

"I'm here, Papa," I murmur. "You can talk to me about Mama. No one will hear. We're all alone—just you and me."

I don't expect him to respond. I tricked myself into thinking he was catatonic or something.

He raises his head and looks up and to one side toward the treetops out in the grounds.

"She told me once she wanted to be buried in the mountains." His voice quavers. "She told me at the very beginning that she didn't want a big fancy state funeral with hundreds of thousands of people lining the streets. She said she wanted just us to take her out into the mountains, dig a hole under a tree, and leave her there so the tree would get the nutrients from her decaying body."

Tears streak down his cheeks, but he actually smiles at the memory. I squeeze his hand. "I love you so much, Papa. I'm so sorry."

"She loved having daughters, did you know?" He turns and looks straight at me through his tears. "She told me once she would be heartbroken if she only had sons. She wanted to share all of womanhood with you." He looks away. "Just as I would be heartbroken if I only had daughters. It is so strange to be a parent."

"Are you still going to have the state funeral?"

"I have to. It's part of the job. She understood that."

Now it's my turn to look away. My mother used to say that all the time—if any of us complained about royal life. She said it was part of the job.

Those were her last words to me—her last words in life. She treated it as a job. She went through the motions and kept her personal preferences behind closed doors.

She never heard my comment about taking up knitting. I wish now that she did.

"I haven't spent this much time outside in years," my father goes on. He lifts his face higher, shuts his eyes, and smiles into the sunshine even with tears glistening on his cheeks. "Isn't it a shame that she had to die for me to enjoy this pleasure?"

"You could change that, Papa. You don't have to stay inside all the time."

"Do you want to know a secret?" he asks. "You can't tell anyone else—not yet."

"Maybe you shouldn't tell me if it's that dangerous."

He laughs and chokes on sobs at the same time. "Geneviève is pregnant."

I gasp and jolt back. "No!"

He beams at me. "Don't tell anyone. I wasn't supposed to find out just yet. She and Christophe didn't know I was out here. They came out onto their patio to talk where no one would hear them. They don't want to make the announcement until after the funeral. They think they would offend me if they interrupt the mourning period."

"But....but that's wonderful!"

He smiles at me so tenderly. "You must think about getting married, my darling. I'm sure there are plenty of suitable partners who would be delighted to get to know you. The Prince of Luxembourg is definitely interested. We already know that, but there's also Amir Baltani of Qatar, Stavros Loukaou of Cyprus, and Prince Anton of Sweden."

I stare at him and then turn away so I won't see him looking at me like that. "I can't marry any of them, Papa. I'm sorry."

"You have to marry someone." He squeezes my hand. "If none of them appeal to you, we'll just have to find someone who does. The world is your oyster."

"I'm not ready to get married, Papa." I feel my throat constrict. "I'm not sure if I'll ever be ready to get married."

The first cloud crosses his face. "Why not? Don't tell me your social obligations are your true love. I don't believe that."

"It isn't that."

"What could cause you to take that step? Marriage is part of being royal."

I can't look at him. "I know, Papa. It's just....I'm already in love with someone and I can't marry him. I don't know how I could ever get over that to give my heart to someone else, but it won't be now. It won't be for a long time—if it ever happens. He's the only one I want. If I can't have him, then I don't want anyone else."

He frowns at me. "Why can't you be with him? Who is he?"

I open my mouth and stop myself. Should I? Christophe knows and understands.

I look up at my father. I don't know how he'll react, but I can't keep this secret from him, either.

Falling in love with Alexei—it was a watershed moment in my life. The people closest to me need to find out that I'm different now. I changed because of this. I don't want to hide it or anything else this important to me.

"It's Alexei Asatiani," I reply. "We got together during the siege—when he took me out of the palace and guarded me in the safe house. He saved my life during the mall attack and afterward. I got attached to him and then we spent all those days together. He's the best man I've ever known, but he's a member of the staff—so it's impossible. We both accept that it can't happen, but I'm not ready to think about someone else. I don't know if I ever will be."

My father looks away and winds up gazing off into the sky above the distant trees. "It reminds me of the story of me and your mother."

My head shoots up. Neither of my parents ever talked about how they got together. I always assumed their parents arranged their marriage like so many other royal pairings.

"Love is a strange thing, isn't it," he murmurs. "Lightning strikes and nothing can ever be the same. There's so much more to love than social standing."

"Did you….?" I stop myself again. "Did you love Mama? I always thought…." I break off.

I never thought love entered the picture. I thought they just got married because it was the thing to do—because it was part of the job as my mother would say.

My father turns around and bestows such a look of beaming love on me that it takes my breath away. His eyes brim with tears, but I've never seen him so happy.

"I loved her more than anything," he rasps. "She was my heart's delight from the day I married her. I thought I could never live without her and now I have to—but I thank God for every day we spent together. I would gladly face the rest of my life alone in exchange for all those years of memories, conversations, smiles, arguments...." He bursts out laughing as his tears start to flow. "Even the arguments."

I don't know what to say. Watching him makes my throat ache. I could have had a love like that with Alexei. I could have loved him as much as that and felt that he loved me that much back.

"I know it isn't the usual thing, but I consent to consider him a prospect for you," my father tells me.

My head snaps around fast. "You will?!"

"Who could say no to a love like that, eh?" He squeezes my hand. He won't stop grinning. "The love I shared with your mother is gone. Now it's time for a new love to take over. I would have been annoyed if you married someone you didn't love."

"But....I can't marry him. He's.....he's a palace employee."

My father shrugs. "Not everyone can be a prince or a duke, can they?"

I blink at him in shock. "You're serious."

He shoots his eyes toward the patio doors. "You better go tell him."

My jaw hits the pavement. He's serious. He actually plans to consider Alexei a potential suitor for me.

I don't want to believe it. I *don't* believe it. It's impossible. It flies in the face of every rule governing my family. It's the one rule we all grew up with—the rule even my father drilled into me from my earliest memories.

I leave him sitting there in the sunshine with his memories. I stagger back through his bedroom and into the corridor. I forget to do it quietly so no one finds out I violated the mourning period.

I stumble back to my apartment and shut the door on that conversation, but my mind won't stop spinning.

Did that actually happen? I don't even know how to think about this—but I have to. I have to do something about this. Just don't ask me what.

Chapter 33:
Alexei

I enter Lucille's wardrobe room just in time for her to turn around and glare at me. Will she ever stop glaring at me?

I can't be the only bodyguard in the world who takes a professional interest in his client's wardrobe.

I've had plenty of male clients I instructed to wear bulletproof vests under their clothes. I don't see that this is any different.

The women of the Royal Family spend a long time getting their hair and makeup done before official events and appearances.

The hair stylists and makeup artists get right up close and personal with these women. Either of the two could pull a weapon and do something to one of the women while they're sitting there in the chair.

The makeup artist puts chemicals and substances right on the client's skin. Someone could poison the makeup to sicken or kill the client. What kind of bodyguard would I be if I didn't check that?

The security team vets, searches, and watches every other member of the staff and every other professional who enters the palace. Why should the hair stylists and makeup artists be any different?

I don't vet, search, and watch Lucille. I mean, I watch her but only because Simone's wardrobe is my job. It isn't like I'm in here to tell Lucille how to do her job—unless I want her to add bulletproof reinforcing to Simone's outfit.

The black dress Simone will wear to her mother's funeral hangs on the wall above the clothes rail. The dress has full-length sleeves, a tight collar that buttons up to the neck, and full skirts all the way to the floor.

The dress doesn't leave a single inch of skin exposed except for Simone's face. She'll even be wearing gloves so no one thinks she's using this opportunity to flaunt her fashion chops.

I've already gone around and around the mulberry bush with Lucille about adding reinforcement to this dress. She glares at me from across the room while I scrunch the fabric in my hand to make sure she did it.

She did do it. The front panels of the dress don't bend except at certain reinforced joins.

I stand off to one side and don't interfere while Simone tries on the dress. Lucille makes a point of asking again and again if the dress is too stiff or too uncomfortable at certain points.

Simone says it isn't—of course. She never argues with my security arrangements anymore. I'm sure she would tell Lucille to adjust the dress if it was too tight. Simone is too practical and headstrong to suffer in silence over something like that.

We go next door and she gets her hair and makeup done. We don't exchange a single word through the whole process, but I catch her watching me plenty of times.

Her eyes communicate so much. I never have to wonder if she still feels the same way about me. Jesus Christ, I love her so much!

It's enough for me to just stand back and love her from a distance. It's enough to know that I'm doing what's best for her. I honestly don't care about anything else.

I haven't seen her in two weeks since her mother died. The whole Royal Family has been in isolation for the mourning period.

Nothing has changed between us in that time. The decision not to continue with each other didn't change a thing. I know it didn't for me. Now I see plain as day that it didn't for her, either.

Will it ever? Will either of us be able to move on?

I don't care if I ever move on. I can just live with this love the way it is.

She finishes getting ready, puts on the dress, and Lucille pins Simone's hat to her hair before lowering the veil over her face. Simone looks as stunning as ever even like this.

I escort her out to the limo and we both get in as usual. We go through the hours-long state funeral, the reception afterward, and then the long official procession of driving the casket through the streets.

The Police turn out in force to keep the population on the sidewalks as the hearse passes. The convoy of limos and cars drives at a snail's pace.

Thousands of people throw flowers and handwritten notes into the street in front of and around the hearse. The Police have their work cut out for them holding everyone back.

I sit next to Simone in silence. We ride in the same limo with Pascal, Renáld, Christophe, Geneviève, and the Crown Prince.

Crown Prince Gustav is much more animated than I expected him to be. I expected him to fall into a semi-coma of depression after his wife's death. Don't ask me what brought him out of it.

He's serious, but he also seems to be a lot more okay than he was when it first happened. I don't understand it, but I'm relieved he's going to pull through this.

We get to the cathedral. Then it's another security nightmare trying to keep all the crowding citizenry out of the line of procession.

The pallbearers carry Princess Jasmine's casket inside. I escort Simone with her family to accompany the casket to the vault.

Then we stand for another long service. Nearly the whole day passes before we get into the limo and drive back to the palace. I don't know about the rest of them, but I'm ready to sit down.

Christophe, Pascal, and Renáld talk for the first time on their way home. They'll be having their first family dinner tonight since their mother died.

Crown Prince Gustav looks out the window with a wistful smile on his face. He doesn't pay attention to anything his sons say. The Crown Prince drifts in his own inner world.

I sure hope he's thinking about all the happy memories he had with his wife. That's what I would be thinking in his situation. Why dwell on the pain of losing her when they had all those good years together?

Or maybe they didn't. Maybe they never liked each other and only kept up appearances for the sake of the public.

That smile tells me a different story. I bet he loved her. I bet he loved her every day until she died.

We get out and go inside the palace. Simone turns to me in the corridor while she unpins her hat from her hair. "Would you mind walking me back to my apartment?" she asks.

"Of course not. I'd be happy to."

We set off. She shakes out her hair and unbuttons the top button of her collar so it isn't so tight.

"Was the dress comfortable enough?" I ask. "Is the reinforcing too stiff?"

"It's fine," she exclaims. "I would have said if it was uncomfortable."

"Lucille seems to think I'm inflicting some kind of medieval torture on you by reinforcing your clothes."

She turns around and laughs. Then she slips her hand into mine.

I recoil in horror and yank my hand away with a gasp. "What are you doing?!"

She won't stop grinning at me. Her eyes twinkle and her cheeks flush.

Her reaction to my reaction sets off something in me. I pull her into her apartment, shut the door, and round on her. "Are you crazy?! We agreed we wouldn't do anything like that. We agreed we would never do anything like that again and that we would move on. You can't do that—especially if you're going to marry someone else."

"I'm not going to marry someone else, Alexei!" She bursts into a hug, blushing smile. "I'm going to marry you."

My world comes to a screeching halt. I can barely make myself heard. "What did you just say?"

"My father. He agreed to consider you a suitor for me."

I can't breathe. I stare at her in shock. She didn't just say that.

She bursts out laughing and grabs my hand again. "I love you—and I want to marry you! He said he couldn't stand it if I married someone I didn't love. He admires you. We all do. You're the best man any of them can think of for me. They all approve, Alexei. My father is considering you. Don't you understand? We can be together after all. This could actually work."

I can't be hearing this. I'm not hearing it.

This flies in the face of everything I ever thought about her, me, us, this job—everything.

She explodes in shrieking laughter, lunges for me, and throws her arms around my neck. I can't tell if she's laughing or crying—or maybe both.

I can't deal with this. I push her off and hold her at arm's length, but my brain won't function. I can't reconcile this with the decision I made not to see her again.

She won't stop smirking at me. My confusion only seems to delight her even more.

I can't think. I stumble out of the room. I need to go be alone somewhere until I figure out what this means—and who I am with those words hanging over my head.

I try going to my room, but that's no good, either. I go out to the grounds and walk around for hours. I don't have to worry about the Royal Family bothering me. They're all in there at dinner.

I sit down under a tree and cover my eyes. I can't do this. I can't be royalty. That isn't who I am—but how can I turn down a chance at Simone?

I would jump at the chance to marry her if she was anyone other than a Princess of Monaco. I could easily have married the young woman I spent the night with at the safe house—and even the young woman I spent the night with at Château des Gennennois.

She was perfect then. It's just that word that breaks something in me. *Princess. Royal.*

Do I have to become royalty to marry her? Do I have to.....? God, I don't even want to think about what that means—but I have to.

I can't walk away from her. She's all I've ever wanted and a thousand times more. I keep telling myself I would give anything to make her mine. Would I give this? Would I really go as far as that?

I'm still sitting there with my head in a fog when I spot Christophe crossing the lawn. There's no doubt about it. He's coming straight toward me.

I stand up and brush the grass off my hands and suit so I can meet him on my feet. He comes up to me under the trees. "Hey," he greets me.

I mumble down at the ground so I don't have to look at him. "Hey."

He turns sideways and gazes across the grounds in the other direction. "I just had a conversation with my father....about you and Simone."

I look away, too, even though I already am looking away. "I never asked for this. I want you to know that," I tell him. "I never presumed to suggest that I could ever do anything with her."

He smiles at me. "I know that, man. No one around here doubts your integrity."

I can't hold his gaze. "I don't know about any of this."

"What is there not to know about? Congratulations. I'm happy for you."

"I don't know," I mumble. "I don't know if I can go through with it."

"Why?" he asks. "You love her, don't you? You love her as much as she obviously loves you."

"Of course. It's just....I would have to become royalty to marry her."

"What's your point?" he asks. "Do you really see yourself as any different from us? You know us. You know you're one of us. You're as good as we are if not better. Why do you think you wouldn't be worthy of her?"

"It isn't that. I know you're all just normal people. It's me. I'm the one. I wouldn't be me if I did all that. I would....you know......I don't even know what I would be."

"You would be Simone's husband. What else do you need to know?"

I shrug. "I don't understand any of this. I don't even know how to think about it. I would do anything to win her. I'm just not sure if I can do this or if I should do it."

"Would you marry her if she lost her royalty and lived as a commoner like you?"

"I wouldn't want her to lose her status....."

"You know what I mean. Is that the only reason? Would you love her as much if she wasn't royal?"

"Of course! That's....that's what happened during the siege. I had to disguise her....I saw her as she would have been without all that."

"Then I don't see a problem with it. My brothers are all involved in palace security already, so that part of your life won't change when you become one of them."

My head shoots up. "You mean....?"

I can't even say the words when I realize what he actually does mean. He's saying I would be his brother. I would be a brother to all these men.

Christophe. Pascal. Renáld. Dorian. Casim. Salvatore.

We're practically brothers already. I trust them all and I know they trust me. We work together, but marrying Simone would make us true brothers.

I wouldn't be an employee anymore. I would be a member of their family.

I can't even think of them as the Royal Family anymore. They're just family.

They've been treating me as family ever since the mall attack. I was the one who couldn't accept that. I was the one who held myself apart and refused to eat dinner with them.

What would it actually take to cross that threshold and be one of them for real? Is that one of the things I would be willing to do to win Simone?

The rest of the family already wants me to. I don't even have to question it—and now Christophe actually said it.

Brothers.

It's already done. It's happening—or maybe it already happened. That barrier no longer exists between me and the rest of the family.

The family. They aren't the Royal Family anymore if they ever were. I've been one of them for a long time. I just didn't know it until right now.

Christophe clamps his hand on my shoulder. "I told her that very first day when she confided in me. You're the best man I could hope for her. You're welcome in our family—more than welcome. You're honored. Accept it. We couldn't be happier for both of you."

Chapter 34: Simone

I'm already in Lucille's wardrobe room checking out my clothes when Alexei walks in. He falters when he sees me and casts his eyes to the floor.

I hang up my dress, go over to him, and slip my hand into his. "Are you okay?"

He nods, but he won't look at me. "I'm sorry I pushed you away. I just...I don't know what I'm doing here...." He looks down at our hands together.

"It's okay," I murmur. "We don't have to hide it anymore. Are you sure you want to go through with this? You don't have to if you don't want to. I just thought you wanted to."

"Of course I do." His voice cracks. "I'm just.....I don't know. This whole thing.....it's more than I know what to do with."

I place my hand against his cheek and lift his eyes to meet mine. "It's just me. Forget all the other stuff. It's just you and me."

"I know," he rasps. "I love you. I'm sorry.....I should be handling this better...."

"You don't have to apologize. I love you, too, and now we can be together the way we both want."

I lean in and kiss him just as Lucille breezes into the room. She sees us together and glares at Alexei like he somehow did something wrong. He looks away.

I let it go. She's going to have to figure this out pretty quick. Alexei and I are a couple. We have been for a long time. She and the rest of the household are just going to have to get used to it.

I change into the dress I'm wearing to the memorial celebration for my mother. This is the follow-up celebration after the funeral. This is supposed to be a grand, formal, and festive occasion celebrating her life instead of mourning her death.

Alexei goes back into bodyguard mode while I get ready. He escorts me as usual.

None of my family treats him any differently than before. He's as much one of us now as he always has been.

Neither Christophe nor my father give anything away about the tectonic shifts going on in our family—now that I'm considering marrying one of the staff. I'm sure the press will have a field day with this one.

We arrive at the venue. The memorial is being held at a luxurious hotel ballroom downtown. Security is out of this world as usual.

Alexei stays by my side all evening. I never take my hand off his arm, but he runs the whole security effort from his earpiece.

I hardly get to talk to him at all because he spends the whole evening fielding messages and reports from all the other guards.

They migrate through the crowd, check out the other attendees, and search the venue again and again for any threat.

Alexei is officially our head of security now. He only acts as my bodyguard so he can blend in with the crowd.

He's the one calling the shots. He even calls the shots on the venue security team—for this and every other event or appearance we have to make.

He strong-arms the venue organizers ahead of time to turn over decision-making authority to him. He makes all the decisions about security both at the venue and outside it. He holds veto power over everything that happens, everyone who works the event, and even where they put the decorations.

He only breaks off talking into his earpiece when someone comes over to greet me and gush in my ear about how wonderful my mother was. I don't need them to tell me.

Our family feels lopsided without her. Maybe I'll get used to it in time. Maybe this is just the shock of losing her. I don't feel any pain or loss or even grief. It just feels weird like something's missing that should still be here.

My father's reaction is somehow so much more unnerving. He walks around with that same peaceful smile on his face.

I know he's hurting the worst of all of us. He deals with it by living in the past. Maybe the reality will hit him like a ton of bricks later. I dread thinking what will happen to him then.

Emeline is taking it the hardest. She cries all the time for no apparent reason—or maybe I'm just still too numb to feel the pain.

My brothers and cousins just keep keeping on. They concentrate on work so they don't think about their pain or show that it bothers them—or maybe I just don't let myself see their pain.

My father stands at the front of the venue next to a large portrait of my mother. A huge wreath of flowers hangs from the picture frame.

Attendees come forward to offer their condolences to my father, bring up fond memories of my mother, and wish my father well.

He accepts all their kind words with the same smile on his face. I can't tell if his behavior is bothering anyone.

I get Alexei's attention by nudging his arm. "I want to go check on my father."

He nods. He's in the middle of another conversation with one of the guards.

They use a complicated code system to communicate everything that's happening. That way, none of the other attendees knows what they're talking about or if one of the guards is reporting something about a particular person.

Alexei and I shoulder our way through the crowd. More people stop me, press my hand, tell me how much they admired my mother, and offer me their sympathies.

I have to stop and talk to them, too. It takes forever to cross the floor.

We only make it twenty feet before Alexei's voice spikes. "Code red! Code red! Code red!"

He casts one desperate glance around and lunges for me. He grabs me with both arms around my arms, lifts me off the ground, and literally carries me out of the venue.

Screams and yells echo all around us. All the other security guards charge the rest of my family. Guards grab and rush everyone out of the venue in different directions.

Alexei barrels through the crowd carrying me in his burly arms. He races through a back door, through one of the coat check areas, and out of the building into another side street.

He crosses an alley, enters another building, and swerves down a long hall. He doesn't stop until he gets to the other end, kicks open a door, and carries me into a different room.

It's piled to the rafters with ancient furniture stacked on top of itself. The mountains of furniture rise all the way to one long, narrow, rectangular window twenty feet off the ground.

That's the only window in the room. The furniture doesn't rise high enough for the top of the stack to completely block the glow of a streetlight outside.

The furniture fills all the rest of the room except for one small six-foot square right inside the door.

Spending all this time around Alexei tunes my mind to all the security implications of this place. The walls are all made of concrete cinder blocks. No one could shoot their way through that.

The furniture would block anyone from shooting us through the window. Even if someone tried, we could just duck for cover behind the furniture.

Alexei sets my feet on the floor and the heavy steel door booms shut. He throws the big, industrial bolt across the inside.

He spins around fast. "Are you all right?" he gasps.

"I'm fine. What happened? What was the code red?"

"I don't know! One of the other guys called it. I didn't see. I just had to get you out of there before something happened." He passes his hand across his eyes. "Phew! I thought it was a threat against you."

I take a step closer. "I'm okay. I didn't see anything."

He doesn't stop me from taking his hand. His eyes lift to meet mine. "I was so worried about you! This whole thing....it makes me so much jumpier about something happening to you."

"Me, too, but at least now it's worth it because we have a chance to be together."

He stares at me and then he takes a step closer. He lowers his voice and breathes low in my face. "Listen to me. I don't want you to ever think I don't want this—that I don't want you. I do! I've just been so confused about how all of this is going to work.....I was never confused about you. I want you to know that."

I burst into a smile. "I know. I love you."

He rushes me and kisses me hard. He pulls off a second later and crushes his forehead against mine. "I love you!" he whispers. "I'm going to do everything to be worthy of you."

"You already are," I breathe. "You always have been."

He grabs me again, scoops me up in his arms, and buries his face in my neck. I feel him shaking all over in that tight embrace.

This is the first time he's really given himself to this—what's happening between us. He holds me tighter and much more tenderly than he ever has before.

His breath strains, but not from desire—not that kind of desire. He quakes with the magnitude of what's happening to us—to him.

I have to be patient with that. I have to understand how much bigger this is for him than it is for me.

I've been royalty all my life. He has a much steeper hill to climb to start thinking of himself that way.

He's still holding me when he gets another message on his earpiece. He puts me down and presses it into his ear. "Go ahead. Yeah. Okay. I'm on my way."

"What's happening?" I ask.

"I'm taking you home. The guys can't find any credible threat, but we aren't taking any chances. Come on."

He grabs my hand, unbolts the door, and leads me out through a series of other buildings. Our limo picks us up four blocks away from the venue, drives us home, and we meet up with the rest of my family once we get there.

No one knows what caused the code red. I'll probably never find out. Maybe it was nothing. Maybe one of the security guys made a mistake and thought someone was pulling a sidearm when they weren't.

Alexei accompanies me back to my apartment and walks inside with me. We both come together in the same tight embrace. This is it. This is the bond between us that will seal the rest of our relationship.

We finally break apart. "I better go," he breathes. "I would love to spend the night, but I have to meet with your father first and get raked over the coals."

I laugh at him. "It isn't like that. He thinks you're the greatest."

"I'm glad someone does." He looks around at everything other than me. "I should get out of here before I get struck by lightning."

I give him one long, slow succulent kiss. "Good night," I tell him. "I'll be dreaming about you tonight."

"I dream about you every night," he replies and blushes.

I feel my cheeks burning. I push him away toward the door. "Be gone, vile incubus."

He laughs and starts to turn around. "Ooo! Wait a minute....."

I shove him through the door, lock it, and hear him laughing as he walks away down the hall.

Chapter 35:
Alexei

I stop on the threshold of the palace drawing room. Crown Prince Gustav stands across the room waiting for me.

I glance sideways at Christophe, his brothers, and his cousins standing on the other side of the room. Their presence makes this so much harder.

Meeting the Crown Prince for the first time as a potential suitor for his daughter is going to be hard enough. Now I have to perform in front of all these other guys.

I try not to squirm in front of the Crown Prince. He claps me on the shoulder before I can even open my mouth—which is probably a good thing because I can't think of one intelligent thing to say to him.

"Thank you for coming to see me, my boy," he tells me. "It's a pleasure as always."

"Thank you, Your Highness," I choke. "It's an honor for me that you would even consider me for Simone's hand."

"Nonsense, my boy," he exclaims. "We are the ones who are honored."

"You're too kind, Your Highness. I will do everything in my power to prove myself worthy of Simone. I'm at your service, as always."

"Stop it. You have done more for our family than anyone." He waves his sons and nephews forward.

They surround me all shaking my hand and clapping me on the shoulder, too. Their touch makes me jump out of my skin even though they're all being so kind and welcoming.

Dorian pumps my arm nearly off my shoulder. "We're so proud to have you with us," he exclaims. "You're perfect for Simone."

"Congratulations, brother," Pascal tells me. "It couldn't happen to a better man."

I can only mumble, "Thank you." I feel myself getting shaky again.

"Now then!" the Crown Prince interjects. "You'll have to meet with Chevalier about your schedule. We have to plan a few engagement announcements, receptions, and whatnot."

"You're going to learn more about Chevalier than you ever wanted to know," Salvatore tells me.

"But in a good way," Renáld adds. "He's the salt of the earth. He'll make sure you're all taken care of."

"You'll need to start recruiting for your replacement as head of security," the Crown Prince goes on."

"And start interviewing whoever is going to be guarding you," Christophe chimes in.

My head shoots up. "What? Why would they be guarding me?"

"You won't be our head of security anymore—not in your former capacity. You'll be a member of the Royal Family with your own body-guard detail—and you'll need to assign new bodyguards to Simone since you won't be doing it anymore."

My hand flies to my head. "I can't be hearing this."

They all pat me on the back. "You're gonna be great," Casim tells me.

"Just make sure you choose the best," Salvatore tells me. "We want to make sure you're protected as well as you've been protecting all of us."

My head spins. "I....I gotta get out of here. I gotta....."

Chevalier walks in at that moment. I can't face this right now. I mumble something to the Crown Prince and run for it.

I don't like being rude to him, but I can't deal with getting scheduled for receptions, galas, press announcements, and all of that—not as a guest and especially not as the guest of honor. No way.

I head out to the grounds again. This is going to be my go-to place to hide from all of this.

I go back to the same stand of trees, but I can't even sit down. I lean my arm against the trunk and bow my head trying in every possible way to steady my racing heart. My whole body shakes with nerves. How am I supposed to deal with this?

I concentrate just on breathing. How did this happen to me? I can't be royalty! That's just insane.

I'm still standing there when Simone crosses the lawn. She's wearing one of her sleek, classy, casual outfits. She always dresses like this when she's relaxing around the palace.

"Are you okay?" she asks. "Christophe told me you were struggling with all of this. He told me I should come and see if I could help you."

I try to straighten up and tell her that I'm all right, but it doesn't come out that way. I can't lie to her about any of this.

"It's just all so....so much.....Your father...."

"What did he say? Did he rake you over the coals?"

I can't take the joke. "No, not at all. He was incredibly kind. All of them were. They always are. They consider me a brother."

"That's great! What's wrong with that."

"There's nothing wrong with that. It's all the engagement announcements, receptions, galas, parties, press spots....."

"You've been going to those all along. That's nothing new for you."

"I don't go to them as the subject....or the object....or whatever the hell I am. Your father even called in Chevalier to talk to me. I bounced. I couldn't face it."

She laughs out loud and her cheeks flush. "Now you know how the rest of us feel."

"That doesn't mean I have to like it. That doesn't mean I have to get used to it."

She steps forward, takes my hand, and kisses me. "Let's take a walk—just you and me—like we did at the estate. Come on."

She drags me away from my precious trees. I follow her across the lawns.

This is a very different walk from the one at the estate. I don't have to hide from anyone now.

I glance over my shoulder toward the palace. No one is following us. No one is watching us. No one even cares to see what we do together.

The two walks somehow merge together in my mind and become one. She's the same person I went for a walk with then. She's the same glowing soul I fell in love with.

All that other stuff back there in the palace—that's the part I have a hard time with. This right here—this between us—this is easy—effortless, even.

She smiles up at me with her twinkling eyes. She's gorgeous—and sweet. I pull her in to kiss her. "Do you feel better now?" she asks.

"Run away to Antarctica with me," I tell her. "Leave all this behind. We'll go give your press conferences to the penguins."

"No way! I can't stand the cold. I'm a snowflake. Didn't you know that by now?"

I find myself laughing. "Fine. Run away with me to Java."

"Java! How did you pick that out?"

"I don't know. Maybe I'm getting low on coffee—or maybe I just came up with the one place I thought would be the farthest away from here."

She laughs along with me. "I might have a better idea about where we could run away to."

"Where—Lake Titicaca?"

She explodes in laughter. I find myself snickering at her reaction. At least I can make her laugh.

She wipes tears of laughter off her cheeks.

"Well?" I ask when she calms down slightly. "Where is this mythical place?"

"It isn't mythical. It's very real. I'll show you. Come on. It's this way."

She leads to the other side of the stand of trees we've been walking around. I don't see where she's going until she cuts through the trees and comes out right outside her own patio.

I stop in my tracks. She pauses and turns around to face me. "This is it. As long as we're here, it will just be you and me—none of that other stuff. This apartment can be our version of the safe house. No one knows us. No one thinks of us as royalty. It's just you and me—the way we were then. Remember?"

I stare at the doors leading into her apartment. One set of doors leads into the living room. The other leads into her bedroom.

I'll never forget the day I first set foot in that room—the day Christophe introduced me to her. She hated me that day. She swore she would ruin me. She refused to cooperate with anything I did. She said I was a disgrace.

We sure have come a long way since then. Is she really inviting me in there—as her fiancé? Do I dare to even think of myself as that?

I will be once the Crown Prince announces it to the press. No one will be able to deny it.

She thinks I'm worthy of her. Her whole family thinks I'm worthy of her.

I think I'm worthy of her, too. I definitely thought I was worthy of her when we were in the tunnels—and in the safe house. I never doubted any of it then.

I even considered myself worthy of her at the Château des Gennennois. I only stopped thinking it when we came back here.

The patio doors mesmerize me into a trance. She leads me closer to the moment when she opens that door and takes me inside—not as a bodyguard sneaking around to roll in the hay with his client.

This is real. I'll be living here.....if in fact I really do end up marrying her. I'll believe it when I see it.

She pulls open the doors to her bedroom and we both step inside. She shuts the doors behind her and then lets go of my hand while she goes to shut both the apartment entrance doors and her bedroom door.

Now we're alone in her room. I spent the night with her here before.

I can trick myself that we're at the Château des Gennennois or in the safe house. I can trick myself that we're anywhere other than in the Prince's Palace of Monaco.

I'm not going to marry Princess Simone. I'm here with the woman of my dreams, the woman of my heart, the woman I most want in the world.

She isn't a princess—not behind these closed doors. Not even her styled hair, her makeup, and her nice clothes can make her into a princess.

She's just Simone for as long as she's with me. She's mine. She's this soft, precious, fervent treasure falling into my arms and falling into bed with me. She's this tender, delicate, vulnerable flower curling up by my side with her arms around me.

She's these beautiful petal lips kissing me and her hands stroking me through my clothes. She's the one pulling my shirt off and climbing on top of me to straddle me the way she knows I love her to.

I gaze up into her eyes and watch the rest of the world dissolve away to nothing. We're alone here in this apartment.

We'll always be alone here in this apartment. We'll always be alone together no matter where we are. No one else shares this. It's only ours for all time.

Chapter 36:
Simone

I squeeze Alexei's hand. "Don't worry. It's going to be fine."

He squirms in the collar of his tux. "This suit is too tight."

"It's the same size as all your regular suits. You're just nervous. Everything will be all right. You'll see."

He peers through the limo windows. We're parked outside another luxury hotel. We're attending it for our official engagement reception.

"I don't feel right about this," he mutters. "How can we be engaged if I haven't even proposed to you?"

I laugh. "It doesn't really work that way in this world."

"It works that way in every world. I have to ask you to marry me. Then you say yes. Then we're engaged. Someone else doesn't just up and decide that, blammo! Now we're engaged."

I can't help smiling at him. "Okay. Ask me right now."

He looks up. "What do you mean?"

"Ask me to marry you. I'll say yes. Then we'll be engaged."

He opens his mouth, but right then, the chauffeur opens the limo door for us to get out. Alexei gets out first, offers me his hand, and holds me get out.

I'm wearing a huge gauzy gown. It looks exactly like a wedding dress, actually, even though it isn't.

The wedding preparations are increasing apace behind the scenes. My wedding dress is a sheer, satin, full-length gown with a few tasteful ribbons and gemstones. It isn't as ostentatious as this dress.

Alexei places my hand in the bend of his elbow and we walk into the reception as usual. Hopefully he can pretend that we're here as client and bodyguard and this is someone else's engagement reception.

We meet up with my father inside the hall. He escorts us around the place introducing Alexei as my fiancé. My brothers do the same thing.

Alexei conducts himself perfectly. No one would ever notice how nervous and jumpy he is at these occasions. He keeps that hidden.

Some people might remark that he doesn't talk much unless someone asks him a specific question or addresses a specific comment to him.

When he does answer, he gives these little quippy statements that always come off as extremely witty and clever. He always makes the other guests laugh. They tell him to his face that he has a razor wit and a sharp tongue.

I couldn't be prouder of the way he's stepping up, especially considering how hard this is for him. He's a fish out of water, but no one would ever know.

I catch my brothers and cousins being extra affectionate to him, too. They all come over to talk to him, congratulate him, and they shoot the bull about whatever casual snatches of conversation they want to share.

None of them talks to him about the security situation and he doesn't ask.

We meet back up with my father right before the formal reception dinner. Alexei ushers me to my seat. He's supposed to sit next to me.

He touches my back and murmurs, "Would you excuse me for a second?"

He slips away and doesn't come back for a while.

I glance behind me. The venue bathrooms are over there. He went off in that direction. Is he hiding from all of this?

I excuse myself from my father and hurry over to make sure Alexei is all right, but I stop short of actually going into the men's bathroom.

I don't find him anywhere else back here. I'm just about to go get Christophe to tell him to check the men's bathroom.

The back entrance doors at the far end of the building burst open just then. Alexei rushes in all flushed and out of breath.

"Where were you?!" I demand. "I thought something happened to you."

"It did." He drops on one knee, pulls a ring box out of his pocket, and opens it in front of me. "Will you please do me the honor of becoming my wife? I promise never, ever, ever to take you to Lake Titicaca on vacation or at any other time."

I burst out laughing and tears spring to my eyes. "Yes! I'll marry you!"

He grins, pulls the ring out of the box, and slips it on my finger. "This isn't nearly fancy or expensive enough for you, but....oh, what the hell. Who cares, right?"

I laugh again and kiss him. Our lips are still joined when he stands up and starts pulling me toward him.

We hear footsteps just then. We don't break apart before Christophe comes to find us. "Where have you.....?" His eyes fall out of their sockets when he sees the ring. "Now? Seriously? You're doing this now?"

I laugh. I can't stop my eyes from tearing up. I'm so happy.

"It had to be done, man," Alexei tells him. "I couldn't go around having you all call me her fiancé without proposing."

Christophe shrugs and waves behind him. "\ I guess I can accept that. Can we go now? Everyone is whispering about where you are."

We go back out to the hall and sit down at the table. Alexei switches back into his suave, smooth, flawless behavior. No one can see anything unusual about how he presents himself.

He gets through the rest of the reception without a hitch. He collapses in shaky relief once we get into the limo on our way back to the palace. "Phew! I'm a mess!" he husks.

"You were great." I kiss him. "Just remember what Chevalier said. We're supposed to keep our distance until the wedding."

"It can't come soon enough. I just want everyone to forget I exist."

"Even me? Do you want me to forget you exist?"

"No, of course not. You're wearing my ring, so you better not."

I laugh and he pulls me in to kiss me. We can steal these moments now because we both know we'll have to separate once we get to the palace.

Chevalier meets us and the rest of the family as soon as we get out of the car. He bows to Alexei. "Would you follow me, Sir?"

"Uh....what are you doing?" Alexei asks.

Chevalier smiles at him. "I'll explain it to you if you follow me."

Alexei and I hold hands on our way down the corridor heading toward the Royal Family's residential wing. Chevalier stops outside one of the guest apartments, throws the door open, and waves inside.

"This will be your residence from now on, Sir," Chevalier tells him. "The staff has already brought up all your belongings from the servants' quarters. Please consider this your apartment. Princess Simone will join you here after the wedding."

Alexei gapes into the apartment. It's much bigger than mine and way nicer. This apartment is usually reserved for visiting royalty, dignitaries, and heads of state.

Alexei's shoulders sage when he sees it. "I can't stay here!"

I take a step forward. "Would you excuse us, please, Chevalier? I'll handle this."

"Of course, Your Highness." Chevalier bows and walks away.

I wait for him to leave. Alexei won't even look at me. He gapes at the apartment with his eyes hanging out of their sockets.

I lay my hand on his arm, but he barely feels it. I have to take his hand and turn him to face me. "Remember what we talked about. We're in Antarctica...or Java.....or Timbuktu or wherever it is we are when we're alone. Remember? We're in the safe house. It's just you and me."

I draw him into the room. He doesn't look around at all the opulent furnishings. He doesn't seem to see or think anything anymore.

I draw him down on the couch and sit next to him still holding his hand. I press it between both of mine. "Tell me about some more of your logic puzzles," I tell him. "You showed me the Difference Sudoku. What else is there?"

"Um....well....." He runs his fingers through his hair and looks down at the floor before he can muster the brainpower to look up at me. "There are grid puzzles that....you know....they're like crosswords except they're completely scrambled.....so you have to solve the code to figure out what the word is."

"That sounds a lot more doable than the Difference Sudoku."

He starts to smile. "Yeah. It is. And then there are riddles, word games, chess puzzles....you name it. It's a rabbit hole once you start going down it."

I smile back and lean in to kiss him. "So where do you want to go on vacation next?"

"How about Hammerfest?"

I gawk at him in disbelief. "I've never even heard of it! Is that even a real place?"

He actually laughs. "Of course it is. I research all the out-of-the-way places I could run away to when I don't want to deal with reality. That's my other side interest right after logic puzzles."

"So where is it?"

"It's a town in the far northern tip of Norway. It's the last town before you get to the Arctic Circle."

I laugh. "We could definitely run away to that." I kiss him one last time and stand up. "Just remember we'll be there as soon as we get through the wedding."

I squeeze his hand, leave the apartment, and go back to my own. It's ordinary by comparison.

I spend the evening going over details of the wedding with Chevalier and Antoinette. There's a lot to go over and then I have a meeting with Sebastian about the security measures for the wedding.

He isn't as experienced as Alexei, but Sebastian is the best we have to take over for Alexei until we find someone better.

I guess I can't complain about Sebastian. He just isn't Alexei.

Alexei is still up to his neck in the security arrangements anyway—just like my brothers and cousins. He always will be. I don't see him ever backing off from that.

Sebastian and his men respect Alexei too much to care about him telling them what to do or correcting their work in any way. They don't get defensive that he isn't supposed to be our head of security anymore.

It's already getting dark by the time I finish all the meetings. The staff keeps most of the preparations behind the scenes so I don't have to deal with it. I mostly just have to give my opinions and preferences on things like the dress, the cake, the guest list, and all of that.

I wait for everyone to leave. The palace residential wing falls quiet. The rest of my family retires to their own apartments for the night.

I wait what I hope will be an appropriate amount of time before I sneak outside and down the hall to Alexei's apartment.

I don't knock. I ease the door open and discover him in his living room wearing his pajama pants and no shirt. He's just punching one of the pillows on the couch and getting ready to lie down.

"You aren't going to sleep out here, are you?" I ask.

"I can't sleep in *there!*" He jerks his chin toward the bedroom. "It's like a museum in there."

I laugh and go over to him. "Would you sleep in there if I went with you?"

"Probably." He pulls me toward him, angles me between his knees, and starts tugging my clothes off while we kiss.

The world vanishes again. We could be anywhere as long as it isn't here.

The apartment doesn't matter. The bedspreads and couches and expensive carpet don't matter. This is just him and me alone together in the night.

He peels off all my clothes down to my bra and panties before he draws me down onto his lap. His skin and power envelop me in softness. I know exactly where I am now.

He isn't the only one who needs to orient himself in the world when we come together. He isn't the only one who needs to forget all about being royalty.

I don't know who I am unless I'm with him. I'm not my public persona. I'm not my social media presence. I'm nothing until I see myself reflected in his eyes. Then I become real.

He stands up off the couch with me still wrapped around him and our minds and hearts joined at the lips.

Neither of us sees the apartment or anything else when he carries me into the bedroom and lays me on the bed.

This will be our marriage bed—the bed where we come at the end of the day to rest and reconnect with each other.

This is the escape. This is the secret hideaway where we leave the rest of the world behind so it's just him and me alone together in the middle of nowhere.

Chapter 37:
Alexei

I pace down the palace corridor on the way to the security office. "Did you check that the security cameras cover the whole cathedral?" I ask.

"Of course I checked," Sebastian tells me. "I checked five times already."

"Check again—and make sure there aren't any blind spots along the limo route. The observation posts should be able to see the whole street and all the surrounding buildings."

He stops in the middle of the corridor, heaves a massive sigh, and turns around to face me. "We already covered that. You already told me this four days ago. I already checked and reported back to you that there aren't any blind spots. Is there anything else you want me to check—anything we haven't already thought of?"

"Did you go over the guest list?"

"Will you listen to yourself? We've already gone over the guest list multiple times."

"I feel like we're missing something."

Christophe comes out of the security office behind us while we're talking. He looks back and forth between me and Sebastian. "Is anything wrong?" Christophe asks.

"Your future brother-in-law is freaking out," Sebastian tells him.

"I'm not freaking out," I counter. "I just want to make sure we cover all the bases."

Sebastian raises both hands. "You know what? You go think about it. If you think of a base we haven't already covered, you let me know and we'll cover it." He starts to turn away and waves his forefinger back and forth between me and Christophe. "Will you please talk some sense into him? He's driving me crazy."

He walks off and enters the office. He leaves me and Christophe alone.

"What's the matter?" Christophe asks me. "We've already covered as many bases as we possibly can. The wedding is as secure as we're ever going to make it."

I glance toward the security office. "I'm just not used to dealing with things from the other end. I just want to go check on the....."

Chevalier comes out of nowhere at that moment. "You're late for your tuxedo fitting, Sir. Lucille is getting anxious."

I groan and turn away. "If I have to."

Christophe and Chevalier accompany me to Lucille's fitting room. They leave me at the door.

I have to fight the urge not to run back to the security office. My nerves are threatening to snap the closer we get to the actual wedding day.

The stakes are all so astronomically higher, now that Simone and I are the ones I'm guarding. I'm not even doing the guarding anymore. I have to let other people do that.

The lack of control frays my last nerve. I don't like this at all.

The truth is that I have as much control over the situation as anyone. I have more control over the situation than anyone because everyone takes my recommendations and does what I say on matters of security.

I'm the one making all the decisions about security. If there are any blind spots or mistakes or holes in our security, I have no one to blame but myself.

That's the problem—and now my future with Simone depends on it.

The limo procession through the streets is my worst nightmare. The car is an open-topped convertible. Simone and I will sit on top of the back seat and wave to the crowds as the car drives through the streets.

This is the worst situation I've ever had to deal with from a security perspective. The ride covers ten miles of city streets surrounded by countless stores, apartment buildings, and rooftops.

I have to post guards, snipers, and observers on every rooftop and in multiple buildings along the route. The snipers have to keep an eye out for anyone who might want to take a shot at me and Simone along the way.

I also have people posted in the crowd, but so many admirers and fans will come out along the route that our people won't be able to do or see anything.

The Army and Police force will do their best to control the crowd, but it won't be enough.

That's the problem. Nothing can ever be enough. No one can cover every possible contingency.

That never bothered me before now. I covered as many as I could and let the rest take care of itself. This is so much worse—now that I care so much more about these people.

I walk into Lucille's fitting room and instantly brighten up when I see Simone in there. She splits in a grin when she sees me. "Hello, stranger," she greets me.

I laugh and wind up blushing. She isn't a stranger. We're supposed to keep apart leading up to the wedding, but it just doesn't seem to work out that way.

She always has a way of slipping into my apartment in the middle of the night—or when no one else is looking.

She has to sneak back to her room before morning, but these last few days have been some of the most blissful of my life. I don't want them to end—and they won't end because I'm going to marry her.

Then she can stay in my apartment all the time. We can sleep in together and slouch around in our bathrobes afterward.

I can't wait for that. I look forward to the day when we can just sit on the couch and have a normal conversation without everyone fussing over us and expecting us to keep our distance from each other.

Lucille is fitting Simone's wedding dress and adjusting the tightness around the waist.

I stop in front of Simone and examine the dress. The central chest bodice piece is much bigger, thicker, and more modest than we all originally planned.

Lucille had to alter it to include an even thicker, stronger, more reinforced layer of Kevlar surrounding Simone's torso. I wouldn't let her wear any other dress.

"How is it?" I ask and my face flushes when I see the way Simone is looking at me. I realize too late that I'm staring straight at her breasts, cleavage, and waist where they arch down to her hips.

Lucille glares at me and moves between me and Simone to block me from going near her—like I need Lucille to control me from tearing Simone's clothes off right here.

Simone catches Lucille giving me dirty looks. Simone smirks at me when Lucille isn't looking. "It's fine," Simone tells me and strokes her hands down her sides. "It's actually really comfortable."

"That's good because you're going to be wearing it for most of the day. Tell Lucille if any part of it is too tight or you have trouble breathing."

She smiles at me. "I will." She snaps her eyes sideways. "You better go see Gideon before someone gets upset that we're talking to each other."

I turn around to go into the other room, but a different man comes out of it to meet me first. He's an older gentleman wearing a perfectly tailored blue suit.

"Ah, there you are! Are you all ready to get started?" He looks around. "I suppose we can do the fitting in here. Then you and Princess Simone can talk to each other while you get fitted." He beams at me. "That will be much nicer for you than secluding you in separate rooms, won't it?"

"Thank you, Gideon," Simone tells him. "You're one of the very few people in the palace who thinks Alexei and I *should* talk to each other."

Gideon laughs and retrieves a suit bag from the other room. He hangs it next to Lucille's clothes rail and starts unzipping it.

"I never understood all of that business about keeping the couple separated before the wedding," he remarks over his shoulder. "You're going to spend the rest of your lives together. Why put it off for a few days or even a few weeks? You can take that suit off, Mr. Asatiani."

I take my jacket off and replace it with the tux jacket he hands me instead. It already fits well, but he starts going around me marking, pinning, and taking notes on everything about how it fits.

I wind up facing Simone while Lucille does the same thing to her. Simone's eyes twinkle when we make eye contact.

"I heard you're on the way to getting yourself banned from the security office," she remarks.

I wind up laughing again. "I suppose I am."

"Do you have your puzzles lined up for what you're going to think about during the wedding service?" she asks.

I catch Gideon giving me a strange look. I look away. "You said it, not me."

"I used to do that when I was younger. I used to plan ahead of time what I was going to think about during press spots, photo shoots, and media announcements while I was standing there with nothing else to do."

I glance at Gideon, but neither he nor Lucille acts like they're paying attention to our conversation.

Lucille turns Simone around so she stands with her back to me. Then Lucille turns Simone back to the front so she's facing me.

Simone smirks at me, holds her arms out to her sides, and turns robotically from side to side. "I'm a ballerina on top of a music box."

I laugh, but right then, Gideon steps away and tells me to take the jacket off and try on the pants.

"You mean....right here in front of Lucille?" I ask. "I couldn't do that."

He laughs and so does Simone. "I'm sure your intended would be scandalized," Gideon tells me. "Go change in the dressing room."

I grin at Simone and take the pants into the dressing room. I'm still in there when Simone tells me she's finished and that she'll see me later at dinner.

We meet back up outside the dining room. The whole Royal Family is in there. I can't stop shuffling my feet out in the hall.

"Is everything all right?" Simone asks. "Did all your appointments go okay today?"

I nod but I can't look at her. I wind up looking at the floor. "They went fine. I'm....just really nervous."

"You're going to be fine." She takes my hand. "Come on."

She leads me into the dining room. This is my first official dinner with the rest of the family.

I already know everyone here. They act like they practically worship the ground I walk on, but I still have to overcome this mental block.

Simone accompanies me to the head of the table. We sit down next to her father. Her mother's empty chair sits across from me.

Christophe and Geneviève sit across from her with Pascal, Emeline, and Renáld in the next two chairs down. Dorian, Salvatore, and Casim occupy the next places with Marguerite, Daphne, and Johanne down from them.

The Crown Prince claps me on the shoulder. "Welcome, my boy. Welcome to our family."

"Thank you, Your Highness," I mumble. "It's such an honor to join you this evening."

"Nonsense!" the Prince exclaims. "It's a pity I wouldn't be able to convince you to call me something else, would I?"

"Oh, no, Your Highness," I exclaim. "I could never do that."

He laughs and the servers and butlers come in to start serving the meal. Christophe and his brothers and cousins start talking about all the preparations for the wedding.

I have been deeply involved in all the security arrangements. I'm not involved in all the other preparations like the catering for the reception, the decorations, cake, flowers, venue, and everything else.

What little I know about it I learned by being the groom. I'm not involved in any of the organization.

I stay quiet through the conversation. Then Christophe and his father start talking about a few other state meetings, appointments, and negotiations they have to attend. Most of them are happening here at the palace, so security is already taken care of.

I've been coordinating with the security teams of all the Prince's counterparties, but Christophe and the Prince don't talk about security now.

They talk politics and all the other interactions, personalities, and scheming going on between countries, heads of state, and corporations.

I listen in silence while I eat. I don't know as much about the subject as I probably should. Being royalty is a lot more complicated than I realized.

I'm definitely going to have to keep my mouth shut around these people. I don't want to make a fool of myself or show how out of place I am.

Simone keeps smiling at me and squeezing my hand under the table. She even squeezes my hand on top of the table where her father and all the rest of the family can see her doing it.

Her father keeps smiling at me. Her brothers and cousins talk about everything in front of me like I belong here. They think I do belong here. They don't think anything of me being here. They think this is all normal.

Chapter 38: Simone

My sister Emeline moves in front of me, straightens my veil in front of my face, and fixes her eyes on me through the gauzy fabric. "Are you ready?"

I take a deep breath and nod, but I can't stop my heart from racing. "Let's do it before I lose my nerve."

"You look amazing. You're so beautiful. I'm jealous." She leans in and kisses me on the cheek through the veil before she steps back and squeezes both my hands. "You're so lucky to find a man like Alexei. I know you're going to be so happy."

"Thanks!" I gasp. "I feel like I won the lottery."

She laughs and I join in—mostly from nerves. My pulse is already racing and I'm not even at the cathedral yet.

She holds my hand on our way out of my apartment where I've been getting ready. My aunt Marguerite, Daphne, Johanne, and a bunch of the palace staff wait for me outside in the hall.

My aunt and cousins kiss me, congratulate me, and tell me how happy they are for me, but we can't stand around waiting.

The servants move in to pick up the train of my dress. They carry it behind me on the way to get into the limo. Alexei, my father, and all the other men are already at the cathedral.

Security guards surround me and Emeline on my way down the corridor. They close tighter as we approach the doors where I'll go outside to get in the car.

I really wish my mother was here to see me marry the man of my dreams, but all of that disappears once I get outside.

I barely notice the security guards forming two sides of a barricade around me so Emeline and I can get into the limo. Then three different guards get in there with us. Two of them sit on either side of me. One sits next to Emeline.

I can hardly breathe on the way to the cathedral and up the steps to the vestry. Emeline accompanies me inside where we meet my father waiting for us.

Another ten guards stand around inside the room. Men in tuxes wearing earpieces in their ears crowd inside the cathedral entrance where my family waits to enter the church itself.

The doors close and my father comes over to me to take my hands. "You look radiant, my darling. Your mother would be so proud."

"I love you, Papa!" I kiss him on the cheek. "I can't thank you enough for this day!"

"It's enough for me to see you so happy. I know you're making the right choice. Alexei is a prize. We can't let him out of this family."

"Thank you!" I hug him, but I have to be careful not to rumple my dress, veil, or hair.

Salvatore opens the door just then. "It's time," he tells us. "The ceremony is starting."

He leaves the door open. We hear the organ music starting inside the church.

The agitation amongst the security guards spikes off the charts as my family starts filing into the church.

Christophe escorts Geneviève into the church first followed by Dorian escorting my aunt Marguerite. Renáld escorts Daphne. Casim escorts Johanne.

Pascal escorts one of the female security operatives Alexei hired to act as the guards' dates. The woman is stunning with waist-length, straight black hair and a slender, willowy figure. She doesn't look right standing next to his deformed features.

Salvatore stays behind to escort Emeline. Now it's my turn.

I puff out my cheeks to steady my nerves, slip my hand through my father's arm, and the organ music changes as we approach the big doors leading into the church.

My eyes lock on Alexei standing at the front of the aisle. He stands with his back to me according to tradition. Christophe, my brothers, and all three of my male cousins split off to stand behind Alexei on the groom's side.

Emeline, Daphne, and Johanne stand on the bride's side waiting for me. I feel myself starting to spiral out of control on my way up the aisle.

I can't see anything but the line of skin on the back of Alexei's neck between his collar and his hair. I want him to turn around so I can look at him.

I have to walk slowly to keep pace with the music. My father's presence steadies me so I don't rush ahead of myself.

I go to our quiet place—the place where it's just him and me alone together. I know him. He knows me. No one else can intervene in what we have.

My father escorts me to the altar and we stop next to Alexei. He glances over at me and our eyes meet through my veil. This is it. This is the moment. We're about to get married.

I even forget for a split second that we're in the cathedral in front of all these people. We're just two people. He's Alexei. I'm Simone. I don't need to understand anything else.

We both have to face front when the ceremony starts. I remember all the mental puzzles I looked up online for this occasion, but I can't concentrate on any of that. I'm marrying Alexei. Nothing else is as important as that.

We both have to face front through the ceremony. We aren't supposed to face each other, not even when the bishop tells us to join hands and binds an embroidered sash around our wrists.

We don't get to look at each other until the bishop declares us married and cheers break out behind us.

I turn to Alexei and we both burst out in laughter. It's done! We're married.

We walk out of the church and stand on the steps to wave at the crowds. Then we get into the convertible, sit on top of the back seat, and set off on our parade through town.

Thousands of people line every street. Alexei and I hold hands between us while we wave to everyone.

Confetti and flowers shower through the air. The noise throbs in my ears.

"My arm hurts!" I yell after five blocks. "Can I stop waving now?"

"Only six more hours to go!" he calls back. "Think of it as a work-out."

I laugh. No one is close enough to hear us.

The car crawls through the streets, one hour after another, one block after another.

Alexei's arm starts to get sore, too. "Promise me we don't have to do this again after today," he calls over.

"Not unless you plan to get married again."

"This would definitely offer a strong deterrent."

We let go of each other's hands so we can use our other arms to wave for a while. "Oh, thank God!" I exclaim. "There's the hotel. We're almost at the reception."

He glances up at the nearby buildings. "Nothing happened. I'm amazed."

"Don't start thinking about the security again," I tell him. "It's your wedding day."

"Don't shatter the illusion. I need something to take my mind off the fact that I'm marrying a princess."

I smile up at him. "You aren't marrying a princess. You already did marry a princess."

He laughs and his eyes dart down to my mouth. "Are there too many cameras pointing at us for me to kiss you right now?"

"Try it and find out."

He leans in just as the car pulls up to the reception venue. He puts his arm down to squeeze my hand.

Gunshots ring out just then and detonate the car window right in front of the driver. Alexei reacts in a split second, lunges for me, and tackles me out of the car onto the pavement.

He twists his body in time to take the impact on his shoulder before he rolls against the car wheels on that side. Don't ask me how he knew where the shots were coming from.

More gunshots smash the car from all sides, hit the tires, and blow them out, too. Broken glass and metal fragments fly everywhere. I scream when some of it hits me in the face.

Alexei rears up on his knees and pulls me off the pavement. "Get up!" he roars. "We have to get inside the building!"

I spin around to stare at him. "What?!"

"We have to get inside the reception venue! That's our contingency plan!"

"What the hell are you talking about?!" I shriek.

"Never mind! Come on!"

He tries to pull me up again, but neither of us can stand with so many bullets smashing the car right next to us. We're safe here as long as we crouch behind it. I don't want to go anywhere else.

He steals a peek over the top of the car and pulls both sidearms from under his jacket. Of course he came armed to his own wedding. Why did I think he wouldn't?

He ducks as more bullets rip through the car body. Bullets ping and whizz all over the place.

"Get up on your feet and get ready to run when I give the word! Okay?" he yells.

I only nod. At least I'm wearing flats under my dress instead of heels. I don't want to run through all this broken glass in my bare feet.

I don't want to run out into the path of gunfire at all, but I trust Alexei. He wouldn't tell me to go out there if we had any other option.

He takes my hand and places it on the flap of his jacket. "Hold onto me! Don't let go! I can't hold your hand and shoot at the same, so you have to hold onto me. Understand?"

I nod again. I don't want to do this, but it looks like I have to.

"Go!" he yells and we both launch to our feet.

He rotates backward, pushes me behind him, and straight-arms both his guns toward the open street. I barely catch a glimpse of a bunch of armed, masked gunmen stalking toward the building.

They wear all red jumpsuits that conceal their clothes. Red gloves cover all the gunmen's hands. They wear bright red ghoul masks under red hoods. I can't see a single one of those people.

This must be Blood Tide, the splinter terrorist group that's trying to kill all the heads of state who are participating in the Eurasian summit. My father is one, so Blood Tide is coming after the whole family.

Alexei unloads on the gunmen and pushes me behind him while he backs away toward the building. He hits four gunmen and takes them down. We only make it a few yards before a mob of our own security guards moves between us and the attackers.

The security guards surround us in a wall of guns and open fire on the enemy. Alexei whirls around in my face and shoves me away. "Go! Run for it!"

I don't wait around to hear another word. I charge for the venue, but we have to run up the steps to get to the doors.

Alexei follows right behind me. He storms backward emptying his guns at the attackers out there.

I have to pause at the top to open the doors. We're higher than street level here.

I push the doors open and see my whole family already inside. They're alone with no other security personnel with them.

I turn back to make sure Alexei gets inside with me. He plants himself across the door and pounds gunfire down at the attackers.

Right then, machine gunfire explodes out in the street. I catch one glimpse of our security guys toppling across the pavement before bullets rip across the front of the building.

They tear up the plaster and splinter the door frame before some of those bullets shred across Alexei's legs. He roars in pain and buckles right there on the threshold.

"ALEXEI!!" I scream and dive to grab him, but he's already falling.

He writhes on the steps trying to roll onto his back to keep shooting while at the same time trying to turn over so he can crawl into the building.

"Get inside!" he bellows. "NOW!!"

His words act on my subconscious brain. I have to trust him no matter what.

My brothers pull me back just as he drags himself across the threshold and slams the door shut behind him.

"Alexei!!" I scream, but my brothers won't let me go near him.

He lies half-propped against the wall by the door panting, rasping, gasping, and bursting out in pained husky wheezes while he changes the clips in both his guns.

Blood saturates his torn pants. I can't even tell how badly he's hurt.

He hears me yelling his name and barely glances up. "Get everyone down the tunnels!" he snaps. "Don't look back!"

"What about you?" Pascal asks.

"I'm coming! Get all these women down the tunnels—NOW! GO!!"

His words act the same way on my brothers and cousins. They take hold of me and all the rest of the women and turn us away toward the back of the building.

We have to pass through the venue entrance hall before we enter a huge ballroom full of elaborate decorations, tables set with silver and crystal, and a huge dance floor.

Pascal holds onto me on one side. Casim holds onto me on the other. They don't let me go back for Alexei.

I twist in their hands to look back. He's just pushing himself off the floor, but he has to support himself against the wall to balance on his injured legs. Blood drips from his pant cuffs and splatters the floor.

He backs away as gunfire gets closer outside the building. He raises both guns to aim at the door and hobbles one painful step at a time to follow us through the reception hall.

Christophe keeps his arms around Geneviève all the way there and leads the way to another door in the back. We pass through the kitchens, through the back of the building into an alley, and into a second building.

This is another hotel. We find a tiny, ancient stairway going down five floors until it enters another parking garage.

Christophe leads the way to an elevator shaft, but it doesn't open for us. He pries the doors apart to reveal another dark wooden stairway leading down to the tunnels.

Christophe pushes Geneviève down first. Then my brothers and cousins make all the women go next.

My aunt, my sister, my cousins, Geneviève, and I assemble in the pitch-black tunnel before the men climb down to join us.

"We have to go back for Alexei!" I hear my voice break. I'm going out of my mind.

"He said he was coming, Simone," Christophe snaps. "Now pull it together. Take all these women and get up that tunnel. Here. Take this."

He bumps into me, pats down my arm, and shoves a small metal flashlight into my hands. "You and the other women have to get away. We'll follow you. Hey! Come on! This is what Alexei would want you to do. He arranged all of this so we would be safe if anything happened. Now go! That's an order!"

He doesn't give me a chance to argue. He pushes the button to turn on the flashlight.

Now I can see everyone's faces pinched with the same worry. They can all see me starting to lose my composure when I think about Alexei still being up there.

He's hurt. He got shot in the legs. He's bleeding.

Every ounce of my being tells me to go get him and save him, but I can't.

Christophe pushes me away and says, "Go!" again. I have no choice but to turn around, gather my female relatives, and run off in the opposite direction.

Chapter 39:
Alexei

I stand in the reception hall and listen to gunfire pounding the building from outside. I don't know how many of our security guards are dead out there. It doesn't sound good.

I no longer feel the pain in my legs. I don't care about that. My mind shifts into high gear.

They're our security guards—not theirs—not the Royal Family's. They're ours. They're mine. I'm part of this family now. I married Simone. She's my wife.

That word does something to me. I can't let anything happen to her.

I stumble every time I try to put my weight on my legs. They don't work right—probably because I can't feel anything below my hips.

The pain is numbing me out. It will come back later. It will come back worse.

I can't stop now. I have to finish this.

I lose my balance and bump into the tables on my way blundering and staggering to the back of the reception hall. I follow our pre-determined route to the next building.

I have to hold onto the railing so I don't fall down the stairs. I get to the elevator shaft just as Dorian is trying to pull the doors shut.

I practically collapse into his arms and he helps me down into the tunnels where the others wait for me. Christophe holds one of our emergency flashlights so we can see each other in the dark.

The Crown Prince, Marguerite, and all the other women are gone. It's just Christophe, Pascal, Renáld, Dorian, Salvatore, Casim, and me.

Christophe comes toward me holding out his arm to welcome me back, but he stops short and looks down at my legs. "You got shot again! We need to take you to the hospital." He waves at Dorian and Salvatore. "You two are the biggest. Help him so he doesn't have to walk. We have to get out of here."

"Wait, Christophe!" I blurt out. "We can't leave yet."

"We have to. Those attackers were Blood Tide. They'll come after us."

"That's exactly why we can't leave." I gulp and struggle to pull my head together. I'm already starting to slip from blood loss. "Listen to me. Please. They were about to break into the building. They'll follow us. They'll follow me. I left a blood trail down here. They'll catch up with us....and then they'll find the women."

"That's why we have to go now," Pascal replies. "We can get the women to safety before the attackers come."

"No." I feel my voice shaking. "We can ambush them down here. We can finish them off. That's the only way to make sure our women are safe."

"How do we do that?" Renáld asks. "We don't have any weapons."

I shove one of my side arms into Christophe's hands, pull the revolver from the back of my belt, give that weapon to Dorian, and take the two extra guns from under my pant cuffs. I give the last two weapons to Casim and Salvatore.

"Casim and Salvatore, you two stand over there." I lead them to the walls directly at the bottom of the stairs. I push them back against the walls. "Dorian and Christophe, you stand over there." I position them against the opposite wall.

"What about us?" Renáld asks. "We're unarmed."

"We can't do anything about that," I tell him. "You two stand by the stairs. The attackers will come down those stairs and move up the tunnel to follow us to the end. They'll pass us and we'll open fire on them from behind. Understand? Don't shoot until they all come down and start moving up the tunnel. Don't shoot until you're sure no more of them are still up there to find out what happened."

Christophe stares down at the gun in his hands. "You're right, Alexei. This is the best way."

He barely gets the words out before we hear banging at the top of the stairs. The attackers are trying to break into the elevator shaft.

Christophe switches off his flashlight and we all move into position. I steer Pascal and Renáld behind me and plant myself next to the stairs. Anyone who comes down it is a dead man.

It doesn't take long for the attackers to pry the elevator door open. They slow down when they see how dark it is in the tunnel. I doubt any of them brought a flashlight.

Light streams down from the open elevator doors. It lights up the first ten feet of the tunnel. They can't see anything beyond that. This couldn't be more perfect.

My vision starts to blur while I'm standing there waiting. Cold seeps up my legs into the rest of my body.

I shake the fog out of my head and snap to high alert when the attackers start inching down the stairs.

They pass their machine guns back and forth across the shadows. They never once think to look behind them.

"What do you see down there?" someone calls from upstairs.

"Nothing!" another responds. "They must have gone on to the other end of the tunnel. They must have a hiding place there."

More of the attackers come down. Those at the front stop there to wait for the rest of the group.

My fingers start to shake on my weapon. I need to act soon before these injuries catch up with me. They're already catching up with me.

The men upstairs come down much faster. They spring down the steps and one of them says, "Let's go."

They all start to move off. No one else comes down from upstairs. I raise my weapon.

That's the signal. Dorian, Salvatore, Christophe, and Casim all raise their weapons, too.

Some psychic bond of brotherhood connects us all. I'm one of them now. Nothing can ever break that.

We all open fire at the same time and drop the attackers right there on the floor. Dead silence falls over the tunnel. No one else comes down. I don't hear any more gunshots coming from upstairs. It's over.

Christophe steps out into the light. He doesn't stop aiming his weapon at the bodies on the ground. He looks up. "Let's get out of here and catch up with the others."

His brothers and cousins step out to join him, but I can't move. I can't feel a thing. I take one step and my legs give out before I fall with the rest.

Epilogue: Simone

I stare down at Alexei lying on his hospital bed—again. He got shot—again.

He lies unconscious with the sheets and blankets over his chest. They cover his heavily bandaged legs. He just got out of surgery to repair the bullet wounds—again. He hasn't regained consciousness yet.

This time is different, though. We're married. He's my husband.

He won't go back to the servants' quarters ever again. He'll go home to his own apartment and I'll go with him.

I want to hold his hand and curl up on the bed next to him, but I don't want to disturb him. He'll regain consciousness soon. Then I'll be able to love him and cuddle up to him and take care of him while he recovers. We'll have all the time in the world for that.

We never have to hide our relationship ever again. I'll never sneak into his room in the middle of the night for wild sex before I slip away at dawn.

No one will ever think twice about me taking care of Alexei when he gets hurt or us doing any other thing in our apartment.

We'll become like any other couple in the Royal Family. We'll become like Christophe and Geneviève.

We'll become what my father and mother used to be before she died.

That's what I have to look forward to. One of us will die first. Then the other will go through the same devastation my father is going through now.

I know he's devastated. He copes by remembering the good times and dwelling in the love they shared, but her loss hurts him just as much as if he let his whole life fall apart.

That's what I have to look forward to if Alexei dies first. I can only escape that terrible fate if I die first.

Then he'll have to go through it. I would never wish that on him. I would rather go through it myself to spare him.

God, I love him! I've never met a man like him—and now he's mine. He saved our whole family—again—and he did it barely alive after getting shot in the legs multiple times.

My brothers talk about him in a kind of hushed awe I've never heard them use with anyone else. Alexei is so fine, so strong, so noble, and so brave that we would have to keep him in our family one way or the other.

My father is right about that. We can't lose Alexei. He means too much to all of us.

Don't ask me how I got lucky enough to marry this man, but I'm going to give him everything. I'm going to make him happy. I have to.

He stirs just then and turns his head from one side to the other. I take his hand and sit down on the mattress next to him.

"Simone…." he groans. "Run, Simone……Get inside the building ….."

I can't help but smile. Tears spring to my eyes. He doesn't know we're already safe.

I bend forward and kiss him on the forehead. "We don't need to get inside the building, my darling. We're safe. We're home. You can relax. The attackers are all dead thanks to you."

He drags his eyes open and collapses when he sees where we are. "Oh, thank God!" he husks. "Thank God!"

"You saved the day again. The whole family made it back because of your heroics."

He turns his head aside and doesn't open his eyes. "I didn't do any heroics. What about the security guys? Did they make it back?"

"Most of them are in the hospital, too. We lost three of them."

He lets out a long, shaky sigh. "Oh, thank goodness! I thought it was a lot more than that."

"The press caught you on camera saving me when the shooting started. It's all over the media. No one can stop hailing you as a hero."

He groans and rolls his eyes to heaven. "Great. It's my first social media campaign."

I laugh and throw caution to the wind by lying down next to him, resting my head on his shoulder, and putting my arms around him. "I have some more good news."

"Good. I need all you got."

"We're married. We made it through the ceremony."

He leans down and kisses me on the hair. "Thank you so much, sweetheart," he whispers. "That is the best news I've heard in years."

"Just try not to get hurt so much, okay?" I tell him.

"I couldn't let anything happen to you. I'll always take any bullets that are meant for you. I don't mean to worry you, but that's just the way it has to be. I love you too much."

I kiss him on the cheek. "That's what makes you such a prince."

He looks away. "When can we get out of here and go home?"

"The hospital planned to send you home as soon as you came out of surgery. They just wanted to make sure you regained consciousness and that you were stable enough to travel back to the palace in the ambulance."

"Can we go now? I'm awake. What do we have to do?"

I sit up and smile at him. "I'll tell the nurses to get the ball rolling. Stay here. Don't run off."

He snorts and I scoot out of the room. The ward is packed with palace security personnel standing guard over Alexei's room. Three of the guards go with me to the nurses' station so I can tell them Alexei is awake.

They get the doctor to come down and examine Alexei. The doctor mostly assesses his mental state, his ability to track things with his eyes, and asks him a few questions about who he is, where he is, and the last thing he remembers.

The doctor tells him he can go home and they call an ambulance for him. Then the medical people leave us alone for another two hours.

Alexei mostly rests. He won't be doing anything strenuous or really anything much at all for a few weeks at least.

That's okay. That will give us both plenty of time to spend together in the privacy of our own apartment.

The ambulance eventually comes. The security team sends a bunch of guards in the ambulance with Alexei. I ride back to the palace in a limo with a full security detail of my own.

The paramedics wheel Alexei into our apartment on a gurney and use the sheet to lift him onto the bed. They leave the sheet under him before they vacate the room.

Everyone vacates the room. Silence falls when the door closes. It's just me and Alexei now.

I tuck the blankets around him and stroke his cheeks. "Lie down with me, sweetheart," he murmurs. "I need you near me."

I stretch out on the bed next to him. His arms close around me and he sighs before he sinks back into sleep.

Nothing can be better than this because he's home. We're home. This is all we need—this quiet togetherness. Everything else falls into place, now that we're together.

End of Book 2.

Keep Reading

Royal House Series: Book 3: Invisible Gem

Everyone finds it easy to ignore Prince Pascal of Monaco. He was born deformed and no one can stand to look at him. He never leaves the palace unless he absolutely has to. The press pretends he doesn't exist.

Monique Bourguignon does the same thing—right up until the moment when he saves her from the violent monster who is supposed to be her fiancé. Pascal knows better than to think anything can happen between him and any woman—especially not one as beautiful and sought after as Monique.

All of that is about to change when they find themselves irresistibly drawn to each other with no way to stop an attraction that goes so much deeper than the surface.

Monique and Pascal can't believe it when they find themselves falling head over heels in love with each other, but hidden dangers lurk just out of sight—dangers that could destroy the dream and cost them the love they both so desperately desire.

You can find it at your favorite book retailer.

Sign Up Once--Get all A.E. Moran's free books including brand new releases

When Jasmine Delacroix meets a mysterious handsome stranger in a crowded nightclub, nothing could be more natural than to take a chance and share one wild, passionate, romantic night with him. They part ways in the morning, never to see each other again.

Prince Gustav of Monaco has enough to worry about getting ready to assume the throne as soon as his ailing father passes away after a long illness. His mother, Princess Estelle, makes matters worse by insisting that Gustav get married as soon as possible—before he becomes Crown Prince. Gustav knows he has to make a choice—and soon.

Everything blows up in his face when Jasmine returns to the palace and announces that she's pregnant after spending one night with him. Now they're stuck with each other for life under the glaring eyes of the press, the Royal Family, and everyone else who is out to ruin what could be the greatest love of their lives.

Sign up at www.authoraemoran.com to read it for free.

About AE Moran

A.E Moran is the contemporary romance pen name for Theo Mann.

I write 70 books per year—and yes, before you ask, all these books are my original creative work. Nothing written under my name is AI-generated or ghostwritten because I write better than AI and any ghostwriter out there.

People don't read fiction for entertainment or to escape from reality. People read fiction to see their humanity reflected in another person's character and story.

This is my promise to you. When you read my books, you'll see your own humanity reflected in the characters and stories. I take this commitment to my readers very seriously. My books are an intimate form of communication between us. I would never disrespect my readers by turning that over to a machine or another writer. This is my bond between me and you as my reader.

I write 20,000 words per day as my daily work output. If anyone with a public platform would like to challenge me to prove this in a controlled environment, feel free to contact me on this website's contact page. How do I do write so much? Find out more on my blog, *Crimes Against Fiction* at www.theomann.com.

I worked as a professional ghostwriter for fifteen years. Now I'm going for the Guinness World Record by writing 700 books over the next ten years and 1400 books over the next twenty years, all originally written by me.

See my website for the full book list. I'm also the author of *Proof for the Existence of God* and the *Crimes Against Fiction* blog.

You can find out more at www.theomann.com or at www.author aemoran.com.

Also by AE Moran (so far)